A Young Woman from China

A Young Woman From China

BRUCE GRANT

Cover image by Shutterstock

Cover Design and typeset by BookPOD Pty Ltd

Printed and bound in Australia by BookPOD Pty Ltd

Typeset in Garamond Premier Pro 12/15

A Catalogue-in-Publication is available from the National Library of
Australia.

ISBN: 978-0-9925514-0-7

1

When he finally got away from the classroom, into the cold night air, the professor discovered his car battery was flat. He cursed the venerable Volvo sports car, with his father's initials on the number plate, and kicked a tyre. It was one of the few things the whirling dervish had left behind and it often played up, as if it knew he could not bear to part with it. He had no intention of waiting outside in the cold for road service, so he decided to return indoors where there was a café offering passable coffee, when four of his students burst through the front doors, laughing and jostling. They all had smartphones and competed to call for assistance, until he explained that he had a mobile phone and had already rung. (He was pleased to show them that he wasn't yet a dodo.) They stood in a group by the car and chatted.

One of the men, Jian, hunched his shoulders and clapped hands briskly. He had a decisive manner and the angular features of a northern Chinese. His family name was Zhang. The professor remembered because it was last on the class list.

"We needed another half-hour tonight, professor," Jian said.

Only the Chinese students called him professor. They were unable to throw off the deference of centuries, he surmised, breeding respect for authority. The rest called him Ian, a ritual established on the first day by the Australian students, who made sure, with robust declarations about the rights of man (and woman) at the first break, that the foreign students understood that this was the egalitarian Australian way. As a result, the foreign students thought all Australians addressed each other by their first names, a proposition that he first thought outlandish but was forced to accept, as he discovered from his own experience that it was true. Even the girl at the dentist's called him Ian.

He raised his eyebrows in what he imagined was a mildly interrogative manner. He prided himself on extracting from classes the essence of the discussion that followed his opening remarks (he never called it a lecture – that was for undergraduates), guiding and persuading, not propounding, but staying on message, like a politician. He, not the students, knew what the issues were, at least for the purposes of academic analysis, but he liked to let them think that they were making a contribution, especially the foreign students who, whether or not they were good students, often brought with them attitudes and insights that were authentic in their culture.

"I thought it went well tonight," he said.

Carefully poised, his response left open the possibility that on other nights it might not have gone as well. The sessions were long, a minimum of three hours to qualify the subject for the high fees for a post-graduate degree, and were in the uncomfortable time slot of 6–9 pm in order to attract part-time students with jobs in the city. There was a break in the middle but not enough for a meal. He felt a palpable inner need by 9 pm to draw proceedings to a close; he assumed he was responding to the inner need of the class as a whole.

"Intellectual property rights are just another way of keeping the status quo," Jian said.

His friends giggled and Jian allowed himself a self-conscious smile. A shrewd debater, he stayed on the sidelines until he saw an opening and then pounced with well-sourced information and stinging opinions.

"Piracy is technology transfer, like foreign aid," he announced serenely.

"And drug smuggling?" the professor asked.

Jian remained silent, although stamping his feet.

"Heroin and cocaine are grown in poor countries and sold in rich countries. Is that redistribution of wealth?" the professor inquired.

The four friends were silent. Apart from Jian, there were two Chinese women, Renfei and Lu, and Knut Harkken from Norway, who was the envy of the class because his government paid for his study in Australia.

"You don't believe in rules?" asked the professor.

It was not really a question and Liu Renfei seized the moment, her eyes sparkling. "Human nature is against rules and Jian is too human to fit well in a ruleful world."

They all laughed, heads back, the sound lifting into the night. Their eyes darted and glistened, their bodies twisted and touched, their breathy voices were visible in the chilly air. They were like revolutionaries, laughing at the flimsy impediments of the world, and the professor felt a desire to laugh with them, which he stifled. He recalled instead magical moments of his youth – verbal jousting, physical closeness, an intimacy that was almost sensual, unpremeditated and without design, depending on no one in particular, stage-managed effortlessly by everyone.

The class had several Chinese students from one-child families. One-child families were not able to do what the traditional extended family had always done, which was to look after itself. Mothers and fathers, brothers and sisters, uncles and aunts, cousins, nieces and nephews – there was always someone who could help, whether it was a loan or accommodation or a word in an ear. With one child families the pool shrank quickly; the single child only half replaced its parents. Smaller families had to be wealthier, or the community had to do more in education, health, welfare.

Conventional wisdom in the class was that China's one-child policy was manipulated by tradition-bound parents to bring sons rather than daughters into the world: 119 boys were born for every 100 girls. The result was unhappy young men looking for wives. The Chinese girls in class called them "bare branches", doubling with laughter.

He had noticed Renfei early. She had an open, earnest face, but behind her eyes was something that amused her, an ambivalence that puzzled, even intrigued, her. She was intensely Chinese, with a strong feeling for family, community and country, yet she accepted that others also had strong feelings for family, community and country. She was capable of holding conflicting ideas in her head at the same time, which he regarded as the first stage of sophistication. The world had become both more complex and less rational, so it was a relief to find someone young who was naturally tolerant and appreciated the satisfaction of balance. Strong opinions held without knowledge or understanding of other opinions upset him.

She kept her hair short and tousled, with a fringe. She did not wear make-up and her face looked scrubbed and shiny. Her clothes were pleasant and unremarkable, although noticeable because she did not wear black, the favourite colour of Asian students. She liked yellow and pink, sometimes together. She wore low-heeled sandals with brass studs, and one evening, when she sat in the front row, he noticed she slipped them off and snuggled her toes against each other. Her toenails were pink. He could see her plump, white knees, close together and inescapably connected with her snuggled toes. He wondered what it would be like to touch them. He was pleased she did not wear Roman sandals, with straps halfway up her calves, and red toenails.

"I hadn't noticed that he was human," said the other girl, Lu, known to her classmates as Luci. He could not recall her family name. All, except the professor, laughed again. The mystery of Jian's humanity, or lack of it, hung in the balance.

Jian protested. "Those without resources need to cultivate skills." He might have been quoting an old Chinese proverb, or perhaps a current political leader, and his companions were silent. "Or their wits," said the professor, restoring the laughter.

A dissenting voice ascended, like a solo saxophone, heartfelt and lonely. "I know it's the centre of the world, the middle kingdom and all that, but there are workers in other countries who need protection." The professor could tell from its nasal twang that the voice was not Chinese. Disguised under beanie and scarf, Knut Harkken raised his voice against the injustices of the world.

He and Renfei were friendly and sometimes sat together.

"Workers of the world, unite!" said Lu.

The professor smiled at the old revolutionary slogan and was about to remind everyone that Chinese communism had a rural base and peasant instincts and had not paid much attention to the industrial workers of the world, when Knut continued.

"What's the difference between a diplomat and a spy?" The hush that followed suggested that this was a serious question, not yet tackled in class.

A Young Woman From China

The professor hesitated. Class discussion was as informal as he could make it, but it was affected by an intuition (some might call it fear) that an anonymous bureaucrat in some airless room far away was kept informed of what was said and, if the opinion was irregular, who had said it. He had no knowledge that anyone in the class was reporting to the Chinese authorities (or, for that matter, to the Australian authorities) but he did not rule it out. Class discussions inevitably developed from technical to sensitive issues, like terrorism, politics and religion. Terrorism was not just a foreign phenomenon; it had a local constituency, weak (he hoped) in Australia compared with terrorism in Asia and Africa or even the home-grown variety in Europe and the United States, but you couldn't discount it. His students came from all over the world. He did not push his own views in class, but he was on the public record with a calmly deflating opinion of the "global war on terror". If Beijing relied on citizen spies to find evidence for its paranoia over the Falun Gong, engaged in seemingly harmless eurhythmics and meditation, why not plant someone among young intellectuals in a course on diplomacy and trade?

"I'm planning a session along those lines next semester," he said, as if that might be enough. It was late, cold, and the service vehicle would arrive any minute.

Knut bore on. "They're both on the public payroll." The three Chinese lowered their eyes, dutifully awaiting the professor's response. It was outside the classroom, and no one except the four friends and he knew what was being said.

Knut was determined. "Perhaps they're in our class." As a Scandinavian, he probably disdained power politics. "Some people might think," he added, a gesture to the handbook on identifying sources.

Professor Ian Ferrier adopted his worldly face. "Spies or diplomats?" Among his students some always wanted to be diplomats and Knut could be one of them.

"Come on, Ian, you know what I mean." Knut would not be put off by subtle hints on career advice.

The Chinese trio raised their eyes timidly, in hope and trepidation. The secret state was being addressed with blunt and forceful words intended to reveal, not conceal.

The professor considered. This meant pursing his mouth and moving his head slowly from side to side. He liked to think he was an ideas man. At stages of his career he had been tempted to move across to administration or even to take the big jump into government or the corporate sector, but he had remained true to his calling. Teaching was an honourable way of earning a living. At best, it had a mission, a commitment to lift humankind from its animal origins; at worst, it provided civilised working conditions, decent holidays and occasional trips abroad. He sometimes thought it would be satisfying to be a schoolteacher, possibly a master in a private school, even perhaps a headmaster. A cohort of young people of impressionable age was an exciting prospect, small and disciplined enough to mould into a unit, working together with a shared purpose. A bit like coaching a sports team, but with an objective that reached beyond winning to character building and social cohesion. He sighed. Universities had become huge and impersonal, like factories or railway stations. The most you could do was to make sure your bit of it was run efficiently.

"I'm not sure I do know what you mean."

"Well," said Knut, "try this for size." His abrupt style left no doubt that he was on the side of the egalitarian Australians. "There are agreed rules about diplomats. Diplomats who break the rules are sent home, persona non grata and so on. But with spies the standard government response is neither to confirm nor deny their activities, even their existence."

"Yes," said the professor. In essence, the difference between a spy and a diplomat was that one acted legally, the other not. Beyond that, the differences were interesting but not vital. Both kept the state informed of what its rivals were doing. They were on the same payroll, so what? So were soldiers, tax collectors and teachers.

"Well, that's a pretty important difference, isn't it?" said Knut. His voice had dropped into a growl. The professor's head swayed back and forth in the face of his student's impatience.

He was not one of those ageing academics who squeezed themselves into jeans and tshirts, wore running shoes, grew beards and mouthed the language of post-modernism, nor one of those in suits and ties who talked about leadership as if it were a skill that anyone with a masters degree in business administration could possess. In class, his jacket, open collar, chinos and burnished shoes conveyed detachment, an old-style teacher, above the battle. Now, bundled against the weather, he was ruffled and human, benign.

"My point is this." Knut wanted the issue brought to a head. "By employing secret agents, who don't obey public rules of engagement, governments undermine the diplomacy that is supposed to encourage peaceful cooperation between states. The diplomat offers the hand of trust, but the spy is evidence governments don't trust each other, that anarchy rules and force, not law, is what keeps the peace."

Flashing yellow lights announced the imminent arrival of the rescue vehicle from the Royal Automobile Club of Victoria. The professor smiled. The role of contingency in life should never be underestimated.

"Deus ex machina," he announced. Then, conscious it was unlikely they would know what he meant: "I'm afraid our little seminar is over."

He was genuinely sorry. Knut had a clumsy manner that would not help him later in life, but he had made a useful point to which, of course, a balanced and judicious response, already forming in the professor's mind when the vehicle arrived, was possible. He wondered about adjourning to a local pub to continue the conversation but decided the magical moment of careless encounter had passed. The students hung around while the driver connected the leads, all of them emitting small gusts of vocal satisfaction when the ancient Volvo jerked into life. Then they formed a line and waved him off, diminishing figures in the silvery darkness.

On the drive home, the professor recalled Renfei explaining in class what she meant by "freedom". It didn't have anything to do with liberty or democracy. It was whether you, as a person, were as important as the people who were in charge of everything. In China, she said, you were not important as a person. You were only important as part of something much bigger than you, protected and managed by people you did not know. Of course, your parents loved you and your friends liked you for yourself, but for everyone else you were just another face in the crowd, another body in the queue, another name on the application form, another bit of data, another number. Another one. Not a person.

"As a person, you are not part of reality," Renfei said. "Reality is … out there." She pointed two forefingers away from herself. "You don't know what it is, but you have to fit in with it. It's like ticking the squares on a form." She ticked the squares. "Or following the prompts on the Web." She fingered a touch pad. "The people who make the website decide on the categories and whether you have a title to them." She paused, her eyes fixed on his. "Whether you are a fit or not. Whether or not you fit." She nodded with pleasure at the precision of her English. "Try to ask a question that is not in the prompts. No way!"

She folded her arms and collapsed at the effort she had made to think and speak clearly in English.

"Not much different here." A droll Australian voice from the back of the class raised a laugh.

"Well, I feel different."

"That's because you're away from home."

"I felt different in China."

Renfei had a pleasing manner of seeming to know herself, without flaunting the discovery. She persisted. What you thought, what you felt, what your needs, desires, dreams were, was unimportant in China. What was important was something that had nothing to do with you, something that had been entrusted to the people with power. History and politics had decided it was important, the data showed it was important, analysis and modelling proved it was important, the media declared it to be important. Everyone accepted that it was important. You, yourself, could only become important if you accepted what had already been decided was important. By people who did not know you.

"Not you. Just another one," said Renfei. Then she collapsed, with her "that's the way it is" look.

"You want to be a poet?" Light laughter in class.

"Why not?" She was defiant, her eyes dancing.

"Better study hard and get on the other side of the door." This advice was greeted with snickers of assent.

"If you are clever, or rich, you can have your own manner of living in China," Lu said. "Like anywhere else." It was bare-faced self-interest, she admitted with downcast eyes, then laughed and quoted Deng Xiaoping: "It's glorious to be rich."

He asked Renfei to translate some Chinese journal articles for a class exercise on negotiating global environment issues, which she enjoyed doing. She said she had a "secret hoarding" to be a writer.

She surprised him at times with her passion and anger. Without warning, she e-mailed him after seeing a film that disturbed her. "The film is about the nature of being Chinese, a people who link authority with inhumanity, who love the combination of beauty and vulnerability, who burn themselves from quietness into flames and who believe that life will always come back. In circles."

Her English had its own charm, content intelligent, images vivid, grammar askew. She told him her grandparents were still "dreaming Mao". Her parents, who had suffered during the Cultural Revolution, were "running dog capitalist-roaders", but were "frightful" about the gap between rich and poor.

As for herself, she supported the regime, which was making China stronger and more prosperous and creating jobs for her generation. The famous Tank Man, who had stood against the tanks in Tiananmen Square during the student uprising and had become a symbol in the West of protest against the inhuman tyranny of the state, did not resonate with her. She wanted things to go on the way they were. Who could say what change might bring – turmoil probably.

She did not have a high opinion of Australian democracy. Supporting in class his analysis of power diffusion and fragmentation in the world after the collapse of the Cold War, she made the sensible point that there were many different ways of dealing with reality, not just two, as seemed to be assumed in Australia, where Government and Opposition provided the framework for debate.

"Ping-pong politics," Renfei said, folding her hands serenely. "The pot and the kettle calling to each other. Black, isn't it?" She looked around the class over her shoulder, seeking confirmation. "The ones that are in Government say there's got to be more law and order and the ones that are out of Government say there's got to be more freedom and information. Then, when the Government changes, they say the opposite. And they change their human nature, like actors. When they are in Government, they are courteous, nodding wisely and listening carefully, and when they in Opposition, they are like savages, shouting and throwing their arms in the air."

She quoted Chairman Mao: "Let a hundred flowers blossom and a hundred schools of thought contend."

She accepted that the kind of freedom she was enjoying, including expressing her opinions in class, was not possible in China. On the other hand, what did students know? They were entitled to have opinions, but whether their opinions were worth anything was another matter. Weren't they supposed to be attending class not to give voice to their own uninformed opinions but to learn from teachers who had spent their lives finding the answers? He enjoyed that.

When Renfei was looking for casual work, he arranged for her to do cleaning for his mother, who had married again and was now Mrs Winterbourne, living in a big, old house. They liked each other from the start. "Mrs Winterbourne is very gainly," Renfei said approvingly. "And not gruntled."

His mother liked the way Chinese women dressed up. "In winter in Melbourne you do have the chance to throw on a few good things." Like fitted coats that swung when you walked and boots with heels. She loved Renfei's "little round face in her pork pie hat". She paused, to find the right word. "She looks so ... thrilling."

Mrs Winterbourne had been convinced for some time that her son, middle-aged and unmarried, needed to "do something". "They have nice figures – slim, but well formed, lovely little bottoms," she pointed out. "And their bright, white skin! As smooth as marble." Her hands made imaginary markings on her face. "They know how to highlight the eyes." She braced herself. "They have good legs, sturdy. No knobbly knees." She contemplated. "Our weakness – knees." Then glanced down. "And hands, of course. They are so nimble."

He listened to his mother with uneasy amusement, as he had done all his adult life. When he was a small boy, he had been uneasy but not amused. Having a mother who other people thought was funny weird, not funny humorous, was an embarrassment he learned to manage by detaching himself, which meant keeping a straight face, staring past everyone and politely excusing himself as quickly as possible. Even now, he never contested her enthusiasms, although he felt obliged to remind her that it was against the rules for teachers to "do something" with their students.

"Pouf the rules," said Mrs Winterbourne, with a gleaming smile and a glancing blow to her son's shoulder. "They have excellent teeth. Good for television."

The professor knew that his mother could not bear television, especially the commercial stations. Mr Winterbourne's sharp-voiced daughter Gillian was a star performer on one of them. But her disdain of regulation included the rules of debate, which she regarded, like love and war, as subject to the superior authority of wit and confidence. She would enlist the support in argument of even the whirling dervish, when it suited her.

It was hopeless to try to explain to her that a teacher should not "do something" with a student, not because it was an abuse of power, which is what everyone thought, or because it was unfair to other students, which is what they thought, but because it was against the wellbeing of the student supposedly favoured. The transplanting of knowledge from teacher to student needed to be intellectually pure for it to take root.

2

THE WINTERBOURNE HOUSE WAS ONE of the last left standing in Queens Road. Its large grounds had been resolutely protected from developers and it stood, like a monument, in the middle of a tangled garden that no longer pretended to be under control. On either side were cutting-edge buildings in concrete, steel and glass and in front was a highway, with streaming traffic linking the city with the south-eastern suburbs. A discerning pre-Winterbourne owner had blanketed the traffic with a cypress hedge and pine trees. Although the address was Queens Road and a mailbox had to be maintained on it, you actually entered from the back, from Queens Lane, which was often empty of normal traffic, although sometimes choked with trucks servicing the construction of new edifices on St Kilda Road.

The gate was black iron and heavy, taller than Renfei, and when she turned her silver key in the lock it opened reluctantly. She had to push it and even then it did not swing open, remaining ajar, half blocking the path. She felt that it resented the intrusion of humans into the garden it was meant to protect, a garden that was so overgrown you had to duck and weave to get through it, its hands clutching at you, its soft hair trailing across your face, until suddenly it opened into an enclosure of bamboo and camellias, basking in light, with a life-size Balinese goddess in cream stone at its centre. To enter the house, you skirted the mondo grass surrounding the goddess, mounted a couple of bluestone steps and let yourself in through a door set in panels of stained glass.

She was always excited, even scared, when she passed through the secret garden and opened the glass-panelled door. She was an acolyte attending a presence within. The presence within was not Mrs Winterbourne, who was more often than not outside in one of the garden sheds. It was a white-haired man who was writing a book about the Pacific Ocean. Mr Winterbourne was a businessman whose interest in the wide waters of the Pacific had begun as romance and was now an obsession. In his youth, he had skippered a lugger servicing islands in South-East Asia and had been captivated by the notion that the Pacific Ocean was unconquerable. Even in an age of intercontinental nuclear missiles, spy satellites and space travel, its vast expanse, studded with islands, was like an alternative way of life to the frenzied activity on the mainland shores and jutting headlands of the world.

Yet the profligate lifestyle on the mainlands and headlands was threatening the very existence of the simple island people. Global warming was killing coral reefs and raising sea levels at an alarming rate. Mr Winterbourne listened carefully to the plans of environmentally sensitive people and organisations, but had little hope of a change of heart on the mainlands and headlands.

One day, he sat Renfei down and fixed her with a severe expression, as if the time had come for her to learn something.

"Do you know, young lady, that on some Pacific islands the inhabitants until recently believed they were the only people in the world?" He waited for the enormity of the information to sink in. "The only people in the world. On a little island. They'd never heard of you in China."

She tried to seem impressed, and then offered a comment. "Like China in the Cultural Revolution."

"Absolutely unique," said Mr Winterbourne, unchallenged. "No evidence of organised voyages of discovery, no evidence of expeditions or explorations. Accidental. People in a boat, fishing, blown away by a storm, finish up on some other island. Stay there." He studied her attentive eyes to see if she was getting the point.

"No imperative. No yearning to discover what was over the horizon. No motivation. No need to know. Just happened." He paused, suffused with pleasure. He liked to wear maritime clothes, like a reefer jacket, and he also liked to seem raffish, so he often wore a cravat of light gold. His pink face glowed above it.

"Blown there in a storm. Stayed there. Bloody marvellous!"

Sometimes he wrote letters to the newspapers, signed "Dr Charles Winterbourne". A university had given him an honorary doctorate and it pleased him to mislead editors by using it. "Fools," he said amiably. He had also been awarded an honour in the Order of Australia, which he had accepted; but when the lists were announced, he had been overwhelmed by a feeling of alienation from everyone in his list and resentment at those higher in the Order, so he had declined to attend the conferring ceremony. Sometimes, nevertheless, he signed himself "Dr Charles Winterbourne AM".

His letters were always the same. "I point out with the greatest respect that your correspondent (name and date in brackets) is ineffably in error in referring to the Pacific Ocean as if it were merely a large expanse of water. It is, on the contrary, a laboratory of human, animal and vegetable life, a veritable microcosm that might well contain the clue to the mystery that has baffled civilisations since time immemorial ..." And so on.

He would sometimes deliver the letters personally, riding a Harley-Davidson Night Rod with brushed aluminium mufflers. He liked to dress up in padded jacket, steel-tipped boots, gloves, goggles and crash helmet and roar around the abandoned race track at Albert Park or weave in and out of traffic on Kings Way.

He took Renfei out through the black iron gate, pointing to a multi-storey construction on St Kilda Road.

"Look at it! Concrete, the cancer of the industrial world! Steel, the dagger in the heart of civilisation!" He prowled up and down, with Renfei delicately in step, until stopped by a worker in orange apron and helmet.

"What's up, mate?"

"You're no mate of mine," said Mr Winterbourne.

Now that she had seen it with her own eyes, he said to Renfei when they were back in the house, she might understand why he was spending his remaining years trying to save the Pacific. People were addicted to all the things that were driving up the global temperature, especially speed, tall buildings and artificial comfort. He was a fatalist. Only the vast inertia of the Pacific, its sheer, indissoluble passivity, would save its people.

In public, he took the position that although Australians were as committed as the rest of the so-called developed world to conspicuous consumption and despoliation of the environment, their footprint on the great Australian landscape was still faint, barely visible once you moved away from the coast. So he used the language of the economists, north meaning developed, south, including Australia, undeveloped. That China and India in the northern hemisphere were both classified as developing countries did not put him off. Sometimes he spoke as if Australia were just a large Pacific island, threatened by northern greed and affluence.

Renfei listened attentively, not mentioning that the monuments in concrete and steel being erected across the street were modest and the polluting effect of their construction negligible by contrast with what was happening in China.

The Pacific Ocean was so vast, the white-haired guru explained to her, and its effect on the evolution of life on earth so powerful that he believed he was actually writing a book about human civilisation, even perhaps human survival, and was convinced he would never complete the manuscript. Her cleaning tasks for Mrs Winterbourne somehow transgressed into sporadic forays on the guru's files, which were strewn about as if the room had been hit by a hurricane. Sometimes she did research for him. This might be no more than a page (describing the voyages of a Chinese fleet early in the 15th century, which he had been delighted to discover) but sometimes she found on the Web new material she thought would interest him. He asked her to check whether eels in the Ornamental Lake of Melbourne's Royal Botanic Gardens travelled via the Yarra River to the Coral Sea, which, she was astonished to learn, they did.

His navigating map was so inclusive and his journey so impulsive that she was never sure what did not interest him. She did her best, folding her offering neatly, placing it in an appropriate envelope and writing, in a large, hopeful hand, "To: Mr CHARLES WINTERBOURNE From: Ms LIU RENFEI." She enjoyed signing off like that. It gave her a feeling of security, being part of a formal relationship. His response was always the same. He would inform her gravely that her important research was making a significant contribution to the monumental task he had undertaken.

Mrs Winterbourne never entered her husband's room when he was not there. It was tucked away on the ground floor with a sliding door into a miniature garden of its own, where he sometimes sat on sunny mornings, under the protection of a straw hat. They were a strange couple, nothing like her parents, almost like brother and sister. They were old, but they behaved as if they were just starting out, on the brink of an adventure. Old people in her experience looked strained, like fish gasping for air. (Or should it be gasping with air, because in water they are not breathing air?)

"Like fishes outside of water," she told Lu.

Mr Winterbourne was a practical man and his wife was a practical woman. They were successful in a practical, no-nonsense society. But the guru was committed to saving the inhabitants of the Pacific from the ravages of civilisation as practised on the landmasses of the world, and his wife, who enjoyed a joke (having decided that life was not to be taken seriously), encouraged him. They bounced about the house like rubber balls.

"Where's Charlie Boy?" Mrs Winterbourne would ask, looking around as if her husband were trying to hide. When she found him she would converse with him as if no one else was present.

"Did you move your bowels today?"

If there were no answer, she would repeat the question, adding his name for emphasis. "Charles?" If Charles and his bowels had done what was expected of them, she would press further.

"And was it satisfactory?"

He would respond with a flourish, as if he were reporting a win at the races.

"Brown as a ginger nut biscuit."

"Firm?"

"As your lovely thighs."

"Good."

Mrs Winterbourne had a remarkable ability to assume authority over other persons' private lives, while remaining impregnable in her own.

"Your daughter has been at it again." In the absence of a response: "She would be obliged if you would telephone her at your earliest convenience. In other words, quick smart, if you know what's good for you."

Now, she addressed him as if she were inspecting him on parade. "Avert your eyes, Charlie Boy." Eyes heavenward, he was not aware she had removed a string of pearls, which she placed around Renfei's neck. "Open."

"Nice," he said, with a nod of approval.

Renfei had worn the necklace all day, fingering it self-consciously. She was not sure whether it was a gift, or loaned to her when she was in the house, or was just one of Mrs Winterbourne's "airful" gestures.

It was quiet in the big house, even with the bouncing Winterbournes, but everywhere was quiet in Australia. Coming from China was like descending from a boisterous city on a high plain into a secluded valley, where the people kept to themselves. Even her home town, Lijiang, which Chinese regarded as a rural retreat, was boisterous by comparison. She remembered her arrival vividly; she was unnerved by the quiet, as if she were intruding. She examined the people at the airport to see if they were different in any essential way from her own people. They were bigger and slower, but otherwise the same. They hugged each other more than reunited families and friends did in China, but she could see from their faces that they felt the same emotions as her family and friends had felt when they farewelled and welcomed her at the railway station on her way to and from university in Shanghai.

She had always been curious about the world. At primary school she learned only about China – the narrative, the metaphors, the images were all Chinese, with a few slighting references to the rest of humanity, especially Japan. At middle school, the focus widened and when she studied English language and literature in her undergraduate degree at Tongji University it opened up, like a spring flower. She had always played the accordion; now she took up the flute as well. She loved the English language; it was "lubricious". It slipped through your fingers just when you thought you had it in your "glasp". Even English-speakers were surprised by it. When she had told her teacher at Tongji he could "beck" her (to show she was at his "beck and call") he had looked strange, as if she had made an improper suggestion. So funny!

A Young Woman From China

What did she know about the world? She was drawn to the wisdom and classic style of Europe. America was productive and creative and full of "stand up" individuals, but it was also rough, even though it was wealthy with a middle class that wanted to be cultured. It was like frontier country, guns everywhere. Africa was tribal and physical and poor; human life had begun there and its people were strong and dramatic, but infrastructure was ragged and civility was weak. Her instinct about Latin America was that it was unresolved, a European manner imposed on native people; the two social layers had yet to meet. As for Australia, she had barely heard of it before her parents decided to send her there, because it was cheaper than Britain or America.

She didn't know what to make of it. It was comfortable and friendly, but not really interesting. The people were like children, happy when things were going well, sulky when they went badly. Australians were not steady on their feet. She demonstrated to herself what she meant by wobbling her body from side to side, and then standing firm and erect, raising one leg and taking her weight on the other, and then reversing.

She was just a young person, but she felt older and wiser than the Australian people. So funny!

Renfei said "So funny!" to herself when there was something she did not understand, although in this case she thought she did understand. Australians did not have much experience of living where they were. They were a migrant people who came from all over the world and were still trying to work out how to live in Australia. She came from a country where the people had been for so long and so much had happened that even as a child you picked up the feeling that nothing surprising could ever happen. There was nothing new under the sun. Australians thought everything was happening for the first time.

The funny thing was that, although Australians didn't have the past weighing down on them, they didn't seem to be excited about the future.

"They're not hopeful," Renfei said to Lu.

"Perhaps they have a secret."

"Like what?"

Lu giggled. "How would you feel if your ancestors were convicts?"

They liked to speak English together, to keep up proficiency. "Australians won't correct you," said Lu. "They like to hear you bumbling along. They think it's cute."

"But that was just at the beginning." Renfei could not connect the professor and his family with convicts. She had been to the immigration museum and discovered that Melbourne did not have convicts. "It must be something else."

"Perhaps they have a hangover, like the Russians," said Lu.

Talking with Lu was like bouncing a ball on and off a wall, the same thing over and over again. She had been longer in Australia than Renfei and had a Jewish boyfriend. She had discovered that apart from both being good at handling money, Jews and Chinese shared a preference for food over alcohol.

"But Australians don't drink spirits like the Russians do," said Renfei. "Or the Americans. Australians like to drink beer and wine, like Europeans."

She mused. "Do you like the acquired taste of red wine?" Lu shook her head. "The acquired taste of red wine is from Europe," said Renfei, "like the cafés on the street."

"Perhaps they feel out of things at the bottom of the world," said Lu. "Chinese are cheerful because we are the centre."

Renfei didn't feel she was at the bottom of the world in Australia. These days, everything was connected with everything else. But the great thing about Lu was that she always said something. It kept you going. Lu was her best friend, partly because she did all the things Renfei thought of doing, but didn't. Having Lu as your best friend meant that you could live several lives at once. She always had pods in her ears, a bottle of water in one hand and her mobile phone in the other.

"What do you like best about Australia?" asked Lu.

"The movies." There were so many different kinds and Renfei had discovered a cinema where one day each week you could go to three shows for the price of one. To show her appreciation, she chopped her hands three times against each other. "I like European movies best. American movies are like Hong Kong movies." She hit her hand with a fist. "Zonk."

"What about Australian movies?"

Renfei hadn't seen any Australian movies. "I love Turkish movies. They're so haphazard." Lu had never seen a Turkish movie.

"So many hazards happening," explained Renfei helpfully.

"What do you like worst about Australia?"

"The beaches."

Renfei didn't like the glare of sand and sun, and men lost control of themselves on beaches. They seemed to think that because people had taken off their clothes they were no longer required to be decent.

"Cave-men," Lu said. But the worst thing in Australia was paying for her own meals. She thought at first it was because her boyfriend was Jewish. Jews and people from Scotland were careful with money. But she discovered it was common. Australian girls said that if you didn't pay for your own meal, it meant you were prepared to go to bed with who did.

"No Chinese boy would ask you to pay for your own meal," said Lu. "And no Chinese boy would expect you to got to bed with him because he paid." As she encountered no resistance from Renfei, she offered a conclusive judgment. "Different culture."

She sat back, satisfied she had accurately conveyed her message.

Australia was more comfortable, Renfei thought; public transport was not crowded (although expensive), accommodation was spacious and the air clean. People strolled in Australia "with languor". Everyone in China was in a hurry. Nature was nearer in Australia. You could find nature in China if you looked for it, as in Lijiang, her home town, but you had to go looking for it.

She missed her family. She felt closer to her parents since she had come to Australia, because she realised their financial resources were modest and the cost of her education was a strain. Everyone saved in China, including the government, because the people knew that the money was needed to build the country. Her parents were denying themselves to keep her in Australia. They never went out and they never had a holiday. She e-mailed them almost daily and spoke to them by telephone each week, but she didn't tell them what she was feeling about things that were important to her.

"Like smoking, drinking and having sex with non-Chinese men," said Lu.

"Speak for yourself," said Renfei.

Lu did not mention drugs, which neither she nor Renfei, nor any of their Chinese friends, used.

"I wore heels to the Caulfield Cup," Lu said. "I was going to have my hair done but I didn't have time."

Her boyfriend had come to pick her up at 10.30 in the morning and she was still in bed! She explained how he was dressed, in a suit with a tie, his hair plastered down neatly on either side of his head, his glasses, which he often twiddled in the fingers of one hand as if they were some kind of toy, squarely on his nose (she demonstrated how squarely by holding her hands up on either side of her face). So she had jumped out of bed, showered and quickly dressed. She always did things quickly, anyway.

"I didn't know what clothes to wear. So I just wore my usual, but with spikes, not my old boots. Or thongs. He said my legs looked sexy in heels."

She was concerned not to look like a student. Her boyfriend was working part-time in a real estate office. "He's not tall," she agreed. "He's not much higher than me, and I'm quite short." She seemed concerned about his lack of height, as if the deficiency in him reflected on her. "I always said I would never have a boyfriend who was still a student, but, well, there it is. My boyfriend is older and two years ahead in his studies, but he hasn't got a real job yet and he doesn't have any money. He doesn't even have a proper car. I mean one he bought for himself. His family lets him use a car, but not all the time."

Lu had an adventurous, swanky walk, and she noticed that men turned their heads to watch her walk past. She was confident and would strike up a conversation with strangers. Her jaunty air suggested she was prepared to tolerate advances, even to experiment. Now that she had a boyfriend she had to be careful.

"Give them the flip," Renfei said, flipping at the air with both hands to make the point.

Lu said that she did not wish to seem discourteous. Also, she liked men, not only because they paid her attention and, in their own clumsy way, offered compliments, but because she enjoyed their company. Men had interesting lives and knew how the world really worked. Women were good at gossip and networking but all they did was retail what everyone was saying, whereas men got behind the gossip and the networks to the nub of what was really going on.

Lu's Muslim student friends looked at her, showing all her flesh in shorts and singlets, and sighed.

"Luci," they said. "If you dressed like that in our country, you'd be in trouble. Deep trouble."

"Like what?" asked Lu.

"Like being chased by a hundred men down a back street," they said, in chorus.

"Luci dear," they said, "Your skin is so white. Don't you think it would be good to cover it up, so that it doesn't get burned by the hot Australian sun?"

"I can carry an umbrella," said Lu.

She didn't see why she should cover up her body just because men were upset by the sight of it.

"Let them learn how to deal with it," said Lu. "It's their problem."

But now that she had a boyfriend, she tried to be serious. He was from a European family, so he wasn't really Australian, and he was very serious. He worried about "bifurcation". He was always coming to forks in the road. If he went this way, he was on a slippery slope, down hill all the way. If he went that way, he was placing himself at a possible disadvantage in the future for having been cautious. Sometimes she thought he was a little boy and she should pat him on the head and say, "Don't worry. It will be alright in the morning."

He surprised her on Tibet. He was definite, his mind was made up. He said that any Jew who supported Israel had to support the Tibetans who wanted independence. Not only was it logical to do so, it was moral. Also, it was practical. Anyone who wanted to keep alive their own culture had to have their own state to protect it. You could not rely on another state to do it for you. They would say they would, even have laws to back up their words, but the Jews knew from their own experience that when something went wrong, they would be blamed. So you had to get a state of your own.

"Jews have had many experiences," said Lu.

Renfei listened to Lu because they were best friends. Her own concerns were different. Her boyfriend (he was her first and only boyfriend and they had made love only once, just before she left) was in China. She told everyone that she had a Chinese boyfriend and that she wasn't interested in Australian men. She had come to Australia to study. She was interested in what the professor was trying to tell his class about the world and what eccentric Mr Winterbourne was trying to tell the world about the Pacific Ocean.

3

Mrs Winterbourne disliked formal dinner parties, with paid servers prancing about. They had no idea what people were saying to each other and kept interrupting conversations, pushing dishes in front of everyone. "They take over," she said sternly, leaving no doubt from whom it was they took over. She believed that informality showed inner confidence and the one thing society expected from its leaders was confidence. Rules and regulations were for governments – and those with criminal intent.

However, she was fond of the arts and liked to employ a harpist and his flautist wife she had discovered playing in the Botanical Gardens. The arrangement was to play for an hour while the guests were arriving and taking drinks, and then for another hour after dinner, when guests were reclining with coffee and chocolates. In between, the musical couple had dinner with everyone else.

"They are good conversationalists," Mrs Winterbourne said. "And they have to eat somewhere." She had worked out a suitable financial arrangement which, without vulgarly deducting a price for the meal from the fee, reduced the overall cost in a socially satisfactory manner.

She explained to Renfei that she would be inviting her sister Dorothy, and the Morewitzes and Burnsides, who had been friends of Charlie Boy since university, and asked Renfei if she would help. "Dottie's no good – she's as blind as a bat."

"My son the professor will be there, but he's hopeless." She raised her eyebrows in widening circles to indicate the boundless realm of her son's incompetence. "Mr Winterbourne's daughter may or may not come." She tortured her shoulders and lips to signify the unpredictable nature of Mr Winterbourne's daughter. "So, if you could ... The cooking will all be done. You'll just be my extra hands and legs." She wriggled her hands to suggest busyness, and then put a plump arm around Renfei's shoulders to show her affection for the underprivileged of the world. "Of course, you will eat with us."

Renfei could not refuse Mrs Winterbourne. In any case, it would be interesting to sit down at the same dinner table as the professor. Lu thought he was a dreamer – "bare branches with a yellow ribbon" – and before each class took bets with other Chinese girls on what he would be wearing – "taupe or beige, with or without cufflinks?" Renfei sensed something more, although she could not put her finger on what it was, except she was confident he did not think of her as a China girl, ripe for tasting, as Lu said all Australian men did. She was pleased that he had given her a high mark for her essay on public diplomacy and had written warm comments on her last paper. She sensed between the lines that he was encouraging her to reach out, to trust her feelings, even when she was not sure what they were or how she got them – although, of course, as he always reminded her, feelings had to be tested against standards that were accepted by everyone.

"And how is your student progressing?" Mrs Winterbourne asked her son during drinks, arching her eyebrows, with Renfei by her side. Music wafted plaintively around them.

"She is learning fast," said Ian.

"Not really," said Renfei. "I can keep some things in my head, but some things I can't."

"What things?" Ian saw an opportunity he did not like to take in class.

"Strange things on the Net. Some people think that the 9/11 terrorist attack was done by the US government itself." Renfei shook her head in bewilderment. "What about the planes and the dead people in them? They say the planes only exist on television. What about the collapsed buildings? They were detonated from inside by American agents to give an excuse to attack Iraq."

"Good heavens!" said Mrs Winterbourne, uncertain whether to be outraged or excited.

"And the American landing on the moon was actually in a television studio. And some people think President Kennedy was assassinated by … I can't remember … gangsters? Cubans?" Renfei looked at mother and son, appealing them to condemn an assault on reason. "Some people don't think Shakespeare wrote his plays."

Mrs Winterbourne, with downcast eyes, seemed to be considering which of these absurdities were more acceptable.

"It is not possible to keep conflictual scenarios in your head in the one moment," said Ms Liu Renfei. She placed one hand on top of the other, and then both hands on her head.

It was not the small talk that Mrs Winterbourne had anticipated. "How interesting!" she said.

"Or you don't have a strong earth under you," Renfei explained. "And if the earth under you isn't strong, you can't be sure who you are. And if you don't know who you are, you don't know how to be in action."

The professor decided it was time to intervene. "You only need to keep sensible ideas in your head. You don't need to bother with every bit of rubbish on the Net."

"I have made a fool of my mouth," said Renfei.

"Not at all," said Mrs Winterbourne. "It's not just what you call the Net. I can hardly bear to read the newspapers these days." Ian and Renfei, and a gathering of guests, awaited the details. "You'd think that unless you've been in jail for murder or mayhem, or at least what they call GBH …" (she primped her lips to give the phrase the additional status of being quoted) "… meaning, apparently, grievous bodily harm, you're not a celebrity, not newsworthy. Unless, of course, you're a footballer or a tabletop dancer. There's a young woman who writes a column because she wrote a book about being a prostitute. She carries on as if her life experience has given her insight into what society needs to be told so that we can all live fuller and happier lives. I ask you."

Mrs Winterbourne encouraged her little audience with a smile that at some stage of her life had been considered winsome. Before she became Mrs Ferrier, she had been Patricia Carrington, from a Western District family that had become wealthy from manufacturing bricks. She and Dorothy, now Lady Gregory, had been courted vigorously. The dreaded Mr Ferrier (origins obscure) had captivated her with his dancing skills. In white tie and tails at the Lord Mayor's ball, he was like something from a Russian ballet, tall and willowy, flowing blond hair, leaps that took your breath away. As a husband, he was entertaining in bed but failed in another elementary duty, which was to make money. Her family had financed the Brighton house, the funds from which, after she walked out, had gone to help Charlie Boy buy back his old family house on Queens Road.

"I don't want to go back to the days when clergymen wrote the editorials of *The Age*," she continued. "But good God! The other day virtually the whole front page was devoted to the family life of some thug who was in jail for two murders, including butchering one of his underlings, drug peddling and women trafficking. I rang up and cancelled our subscription. I gave whoever it was a piece of my mind. I said *The Age* was abdicating its position of leadership in the community. How did they expect young people to behave when it was clear you could get yourself on the telly or the front page by living a low life and then bragging about it? It's bad enough having pop stars and footballers all over the place, with their deceptive good looks, but when the dregs are given top billing, I give up."

The entire company had now gathered and a round of applause followed, which Mrs Winterbourne received with a modest inclination of her head, before inviting her guests to be seated at the dinner table. She and Renfei then delivered the entrée – tamarind chicken, with bean sprouts, slices of pear, shallots and herbs.

"What are they trying to do?" she asked, taking her seat. "Destroy our society?"

All the guests except Renfei knew that Mrs Winterbourne was able to swing from irreverent libertarian to stalwart defender of the established order without missing a beat, so she looked to Renfei for support. "You don't have that sort of nonsense in China, do you?"

"Crime in China is under control," said Renfei, wiping her mouth delicately with a hand-crocheted napkin. "Although, since China became a business, money fraud is leaping like a kangaroo."

The napkin became suddenly an object of interest. "They're lovely, Patty," said Cathy

Burnside. "Where did you get them?" Mrs Winterbourne waved one hand airily, as if she did not know or had forgotten.

She had a weakness, which was joked about in family circles and among close friends. She was a shoplifter or as her friends said, light-fingered, or as she herself admitted, "unable to resist the appeal of small and inconsequential things." Her habit was so persistent that she admitted it was an addiction. It began when she was young, when she stole to be daring. It took a grip during her first marriage when she was under the influence of Ayn Rand, believing that creative people were not obliged to obey the rules. That she was not herself creative did not prevent her from applying the maxim to herself. She embraced freedom as a form of protest, although she herself never protested publicly about anything.

Charlie Boy treated Patty's weakness as one of her little tricks, like pretending to be fond of young people while actually hating them for reminding her of lost opportunities, or refusing to have toast with breakfast because eating it was noisy. His attitude to marriage was seigneurial. He accepted it, and the Mrs Winterbournes, as both complement and compliment to the depth, breadth and generosity of his personality.

"You should have a talk with your professor," Mrs Winterbourne said to Renfei. "He's good at silly ideas." She smiled sweetly. "Just the two of you. Tete-a-tete."

All the women at the table turned their eyes towards Professor Ian Ferrier, the known misogynist negotiating middle age. They then turned their eyes towards Ms Liu Renfei, the young woman from China who seemed to occupy some kind of position of trust in the Winterbourne household. They then turned to their hostess, expecting a connection.

"Don't look at me," Patricia Winterbourne nee Carrington protested. "I'm the last person in the world to know what's going on." She glared at her husband, inviting him to pick up the glove she had gallantly thrown in his path. But other thoughts were shadowing Charlie Boy's mind.

"Whether it's a tsunami, an earthquake, a suicide bomber, an improvised explosive device or a nuclear bomb, the effect is the same," he said. Aware that he had the attention of the table, he released a prepared line in a booming, prophetic voice. "Multi-storeyed buildings are doomed. Pacific islanders in thatched huts are better off."

Marty Morewitz, who built big buildings and lived in one, pricked up his ears. "But global warming will swamp the islanders with rising seas." His soft eyes belied a sharp mind.

Dr Charles Winterbourne, AM, then surveyed the table as if it were a board meeting facing a difficult decision. "The industrial world has the fate of the rest of the world in the palm of its hand. Or should I say, in the crate, or should it be the cage, or perhaps the cradle, anyway the driver's seat, of the crane, the symbol of industrial progress. It is industry that pollutes the air, industry that builds the skyscrapers that trap us under them when the inevitable happens and the earth rebels against its treatment and brushes us from its face, like we brush away flies and ants."

"Suicide bombers will still be there, whether we pollute the air or not." Marty thought a lot about suicide bombers.

"They are a symptom of a world that has lost its way in the pursuit of speed and wealth." Genial Dr Winterbourne had a diagnosis for everything, while keeping prognosis to himself. "Modern man has lost sight of the fact that he is part of nature. He has become so proud of himself for conquering nature that he has forgotten who he is, created in the image of God as part of nature."

Marty pounced. "When did you become religious?"

A streak of irony in Marty had with age become detachment, from the resilient heights of which he observed the passing parade of life's movers and shakers. What would have seemed cynicism in a young man was now wry, deflationary humour, admired by Australians. He was fascinated with the market and liked to sit out on his balcony in the morning, observing cars, trucks, trams, buses, bicyclists and pedestrians converging on the city, knowing that it would disgorge them with similar efficiency at the end of the day. The market's elegant equation of supply and demand was like a creation of nature.

Charlie Boy had not meant to sound religious, so he made a joke of it. "Those old Hebrews were right about the Garden of Eden, but they got the wrong address. They weren't aware of the Pacific Ocean."

Through groans at the table, John Burnside could be heard trying to ask a serious question. He was a man of the world, and he knew that the one certainty in political life was that the rich would prey on the poor and the weak would never inherit the earth. Also, that man-made law, in all its majestic impartiality (to quote Anatole France), would forbid the rich as well as the poor to sleep under bridges, beg in the streets and steal bread.

"You want to revert to shared poverty? Sell all your shares? Grow your own fruit and vegies? Shop at the corner store? Ride a bike?" Murmur around the table suggested that a good number wished to do all those things, while refusing to accept that this placed them in a state of impoverishment.

Johnno was the only one of the three friends with political connections, although no one was sure with which party. He had been seen lunching at restaurants at the top end of Bourke Street with former Liberal and Labor premiers. He was known to vote differently at each level of government, preferring Labor at the national level and various shades from conservative to green at state and local levels. His theory was that Labor, the party of the aspiring lower classes, was more easily seduced and corrupted by money, which was difficult at the abstract level of national politics, isolated from the real world in the bureaucratic fortress of Canberra, while the cities and regional towns were full of dodgy characters who could smell a suppurating politician like flies could sniff a carcase. Lobbyists had congregated in Canberra and it remained a truism that, at least at election time, all politics were local, but the temptations at national level were more intellectual and strategic, less personal and crudely material. Also, Labor was more innovative at national level. The conservatives relied on bedrock notions of security and prosperity. Labor was prepared to have a go at expressing what it meant to be an Australian.

The republic, for example. Johnno was a dyed-in-the-wool republican. Australia had a constitution that no longer represented the sentiment of the people but because it could only be changed by referendum – and the terms of success in a referendum, requiring a majority of votes in a majority of states, made this difficult – the conservatives were always tempted to oppose change. It was politically easier than designing a new constitution.

When they were students, Johnno had been mocked for a lock of hair that fell across his brow, turning him into a romantic who everyone (including himself) predicted would die young, full of heroic thoughts and progressive ideas, sadly unattainable. Now he railed against the glorification of youth in advertising and the media, the use of beautiful bodies and fresh faces to sell products that had no social value and might even be harmful.

"Satyagraha!" said Charlie Boy. When he was confident from the silence that he had everyone's attention, he explained. "Literally, grasp of truth, better known as non-violent resistance. Civil disobedience. Evolutionary change. Better than revolution. Revolution gives the authorities the moral right to use force."

"Gandhi and his wife were married when they were thirteen." Johnno, the source of this information, drily surveyed the guests, as if satyagraha's credentials had been demolished.

Mrs Winterbourne rose to her feet, reminding her guests that this was a dinner party, not a debating society. Sighs of appreciation acknowledged that the delicate entrée had been duly despatched. Renfei gathered the plates while the lady of the house departed to the kitchen. They returned with larger plates of roast lamb, with peas, pumpkin and baked potato.

"I would like our musical guests to tell us what they were so beautifully playing when you all arrived," said the hostess.

But the flautist was aching to tell everyone about a trip she had made recently to China. She would like to ask everyone to try to answer a question.

"Why can't we be more like the Chinese?"

It was an unexpected sentiment in the secluded room, the diners busy around the mahogany table. A muffled grumbling indicated some general sympathy with the questioner.

"The Chinese are remarkable people." The traveller had returned with a very clear impression of one-fifth of human kind.

Wise noddings. Forks, inserted precisely into mouths, caused barely a clink of metal on enamel. Eyes remained lowered, noting obliquely the silver salt and pepper shakers and the bowl of floating marigold heads, or suddenly scanned the embossed wallpaper, or darted up to an ornamental cornice, or swept down to a ringed finger. Or glanced surreptitiously in Renfei's direction.

"The lamb is delicious."

"They're very well organised," said the flautist. Her wide blue eyes roamed artlessly around the table. Her husband, the harpist, whispered to his companion, Cathy Burnside, that he had heard it all before. Before the dinner party, or the journey to China that had preceded it, she had not been known to hold views about the organisation of society.

From the lowered heads came a mumbling. "A bit of organisation wouldn't go astray here." And: "We're at sixes and sevens." The mumbling became a rumbling, a metaphor for anxiety, whether over taxes, unemployment, terrorism, the price of fuel, global warming or the torture and slaughter of so many people in so many parts of the world was unclear. There was also mounting evidence that children were obsessed with money and sex at rapidly descending ages.

"And they're so courteous."

The discourtesies of life in Australia were legendary. Even in Hobart, manners were deteriorating.

With a humorous shake of long hair, the harpist eyed his wife above the flashing utensils. "Not much choice." She pondered, her recently acquired knowledge forming lines of wistful authority around her mouth. "I don't follow."

"Well, there's so many of them." He had the decency to look at Renfei, but tossed his head nevertheless.

Everyone was aware of Renfei. The professor was thinking about her plump knees and wondering what she would be like when she emerged from her student chrysalis. Marty was observing her with hooded eyes, assessing her intentions in the Winterbourne family. Johnno noticed a forthright, earnest young person who, with the right preparation, could become a useful aide to some public figure. Evie Morewitz reflected on her facial bone structure and slender fingers. Cathy Burnside caught her breath. She had had an affair at university with a budding politician, killed in a car accident, and looking at Renfei recalled a moment in her life when she had seemed on the brink of changing the world. Lady Gregory smiled vacantly in Renfei's direction and ate the food placed before her.

"We went on a train, quite a long journey," the flautist said evenly. "You could see whatever you wanted through the windows. There was plenty of land. A few more people than you see in the Australian countryside, but plenty of land."

Her head-tossing husband concentrated on a potato, which from his expression might have been melting in his mouth.

"I wasn't thinking of just the Chinese. You could say the same for the Japanese – or the Javanese." Pleased at the twist, he went no further, although a lull in the conversation might have suggested a need.

Dr Charles Winterbourne, AM, sat back in his chair. "The relationship of people to land is vital. Australia has space – that's what gives us our freedom. Asians have different values from us because their attitude to land is different, more protective." He changed tack. "We might have space, but we still like to live in terrace houses, copied from the English on their crowded little island, and multi-storeyed buildings, copied from the Americans." He did not expect a response. It was enough to reveal one of life's many engaging contradictions.

"Are you saying we should stop Asian immigration?"

Evie Morewitz was active in voluntary work with refugees. Also, since their daughter, Verya, had been seeing the Burnside boy, Matthew, she had taken more notice of Australian politics, as it was assumed that the son of John Burnside could not evade his genetic duties.

"Not at all." Mr Winterbourne was profusely sensitive to her tone of voice. "Not at all." Yet he was disinclined to advance the conversation. "Not at all."

"We must bring in enough non-Europeans to show that we are not racist, but not enough to show that we are."

This was recited by Professor Ian Ferrier, to light, approving laughter. "I read it somewhere."

"Not bad." A rueful wagging of harpist hair.

"A cop-out." Mrs Morewitz turned to the flautist. "Don't you agree?"

The traveller responded perceptibly to the pressure in the woman's voice, but did not speak.

"They're great migrants," Charlie Boy declared. "I mean historically. They're all over the world. Not just here. Why should they stop? They don't need to have reasons. They just come. If they make a good life for themselves, they stay."

"They'll stop if you stop 'em." Johnno, familiar with minds of movers and shakers, was not inclined to remain inconspicuous any longer.

"Well …" A chirp, really, from the hostess. "What a dry autumn we're having!"

"Lovely lamb," said Lady Dorothy, munching delicately. She smiled to herself as people exposed their ignorance and bad manners. She had been delivered to the house in Queens Road by Charlie Boy and would be returned by him, unless one of the guests offered, which was unlikely. Except for Renfei, they all lived nearby and might even be walking home.

Charlie Boy wondered if he could ask Renfei to take Dottie home in a taxi. He had, however, more wisdom to impart. He had once been in the business of building bridges and tunnels and had built them in both India and China before he had seen the light and stopped trying to vanquish nature. The bridges and tunnels were more or less the same, but the builders were very different people to do business with.

"Indians are legalistic. They want contracts as thick as my wrist." He showed how thick his wrist was. "They argue over every comma. It's as if they don't trust anyone, including the legal system, and they need a document that's foolproof."

"And the Chinese?" asked the traveller, keen to return to her favourite topic.

"The opposite. A wink and a nod will do, perhaps a shake of the hand. They want to get on with the job. Of course, the money has to be upfront. If the money's there, the job is done. No questions asked." He gleamed around the table. "That's all. Very easy to do business with, the Chinese."

The voyager smiled her appreciation. "It's because they are living profoundly."

Her words lingered over the table. No one could match the intensity of whatever it was that had happened to her, except perhaps her husband. "You'd go mad if you had to live like that."

"Like what?" He had not made the journey. "Well, you said yourself when you got back, everything was under wraps."

"I said there was a strong sense of discipline."

"And when did you become a lover of discipline?"

As the guests savoured the implications of this marital exchange, the hostess prematurely delivered the sweets, placing a bowl of white chocolate and macadamia baklava, with Turkish delight ice-cream and date brûlée, before each of the guests. Her sweets were always a talking point. Memories had been stirred, however, at the head of the table.

Charlie Boy boomed the following information: "Quote. One-child families are actively encouraged. On the other hand, as China remains a peasant country, male children are still in favour. So there has been a rise in the use of gender diagnosis and abortion, if the foetus is female, and a revival of the custom of drowning baby girls. Unquote."

"That can't be right." Evie, the flautist's friend, managed to hold the note of scepticism in her voice.

"I'm sure it's more complex than that." The flautist was an intrepid discoverer, a voyager, even a pilgrim, but not a sociologist. She had found since she returned that complexity was protective. "They're very community-minded."

Renfei caught the professor's eye and demurely lowered hers. She had no desire to enter the argument, but felt obliged to say something.

"I'm a one-child family."

Conversation stopped short, then erupted in small retorts: "Really!" and "How do you feel?" and "Of course" and "In person". The diners smiled contentedly at the phenomenon in their midst, but took their appreciation no further.

"I knew someone who went to live in a kibbutz in Israel," said Cathy Burnside. "You remember her, Truby something or other. She couldn't take it. She said it was exciting at first, hands in the soil, carrying water from the well as they did in Biblical times, applying the latest in science, like solar power. And sharing everything, not just housing, income. The common wealth." She looked eagerly around the table. "Everyone thought they were building a new world. But then ... She said it lacked, well ..."

"What?"

"Charm, I think she said."

"Charm!" The head-tosser transferred his support to the traveller, his good wife.

"Well … perhaps charm isn't the right word. But what's it all for, slaving away in the sun, having you own little row of beans?" Weakening, she laughed in defeat. "You know what I mean."

"I'd rather go to Noosa," said Marty, with a recollected touch of suavity.

"Noosa's awful!" It was a chorus. "It's almost as bad as Surfers."

Johnno's mind had settled on a geo-political convention. "We need the Chinese to stop the Russians – or the Japanese. Or the Americans! Checks and balances, balance of power. Let them cancel each other out, so we're sitting pretty."

"That's politics," said the flautist unhappily. "I'm not interested in politics."

"It's not politics." Johnno faced the issue unflinchingly. "It's life and death. All this space. Don't tell me the Japanese don't still look south with envious eyes."

Marty turned up his nose at the mention of life and death. "Bread and butter, more likely. It's a massive market, if you can get in."

Johnno deferred to the world of business. "Are you in?"

"Not me!" Hands in the air. "It's not that easy. You can't just think of something that no Chinese female can resist and expect to be an instant millionaire!"

"Is the currency firm?"

"Tight as a drum. The boys in Beijing are good Marxists, no nonsense about a clean float and free trade."

The flautist, watching, said softly: "Of course, it's personal, isn't it, the way we see things." Her eyes wandered to her new friend. "You don't think I could do it?"

Her friend's smile quivered above a hubbub that had broken out over the harpist's claim that the Chinese were even more conspicuous consumers than the Americans. Wealthy Chinese loved showing off, he said, with even less discretion than the Americans. The British in Hong Kong had kept them under aesthetic control, while exploiting their commercial instincts, and in Taiwan they were still under the influence of the conservative Kuomintang, but on the mainland they were becoming rich and no one was stopping them. The sky was the limit. Bad taste was rampant.

"I don't think he likes Chinese music," Ian whispered to Renfei. He felt her need for support as her country was dismembered.

"Do what?" asked the flautist's friend across the table.

"Learn to live ... more profoundly."

The two women stared at each other. Evie Morewitz got up quickly from her chair and edged herself around the tilted backs and busy heads, slipping her arm along the flautist's shoulder, touching a cheek with her lips. "Of course you could."

Charlie Boy stood to announce that the wines they had been drinking were, both red and white, from the Yarra Valley, Australia's premier boutique vineyard. He then suggested a move to the historic drawing room, where the couple who had entertained the dinner table with their conversation would now engage the "sensual imagination" of guests with their musical talent.

The party lapsed into something resembling normality, clusters forming after the musical couple packed their instruments and departed, the male triumvirate on one side and the women on the other, Lady Gregory smiling into space and the professor darting from one side to the other. A decision was somehow taken to save a small, struggling theatre. Marty and Evie would harass wealthy Jewish friends, Johnno and Cathy would prevail on politicians and highly placed public servants, Charlie and Patty would allow themselves to be interviewed, as notable Melbourne eccentrics, in the relevant free suburban newspaper. The two of us!

Renfei was too busy for the rest of the evening to take notice. From the kitchen, she could hear only a muffled undertone, with breaks of laughter. She tried to place the professor and his strange circle. They seemed to think that whatever they thought was right, and that the government would inevitably come to think the same. In China, it was the other way around. The government decided, and then the elite (which she supposed the professor's circle was) had to determine whether it would support, whole or half-heartedly, what had been decided.

No one spoke as if the government knew more, had more facts, more models, more analysis at its disposal, not to mention the power to deal disagreeably with anyone who disputed its authority. No one seemed to think they should consult the authorities before offering an opinion. They just came out with whatever was in their heads. On "tip of tongue". So funny!

Perhaps, Renfei pondered as she washed dishes, if you "let your steam go" in conversations at dinner tables and in letters to the newspapers, you did not need to revolt. And the police and the military did not need to be on the alert all the time for people who were secretly planning to revolt.

She asked Lu, who said her boyfriend wanted to revolt but did not know how to go about it. So many people were marching against something, who would notice him standing in the street with a placard Down with Handicapping Horse Racing? Her boyfriend was passionate about horses and thought it was unfair that the more successful they were, the heavier the load they had to carry. It was penalising talent in favour of closer finishes, so that the public could be excited. It only benefited the bookmakers and those who knew how to assess form and manipulate the odds. And television, of course.

"What's it like having a Jewish boyfriend?" Renfei asked.

"He's human," said Lu. "All his bits are in the right places."

"Does it bother you he thinks he's one of God's chosen people."

"He's not religious."

"But culturally?"

"He laughs about culture. His dad told him when he was young that Chinese girls' pussies pointed the other way."

Renfei said she couldn't imagine being in love with a non-Chinese man. Then, having said it, she corrected herself. "If he was a Christian or a Muslim, or someone who believed that, if you weren't, you were going to hell."

Lu said if he loved you, he wouldn't think like that. Renfei said he might love you but secretly he would think like that and after a while it wouldn't work. Lu said that after a while lots of relationships didn't work. Renfei said if you had the same culture there was more chance you could work things out. Lu said that men were attracted to foreign women while women preferred the security of their own kind, and that put them at a disadvantage, gave them less choice. Renfei said with a population of more than one billion, there was plenty of choice in China. Lu said Chinese men were arrogant, did not know how to make women happy. Renfei said women should know how to be happy themselves, not have to rely on men.

"You're a feminist!" said Lu, delighted with her friend.

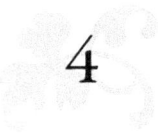

4

THE PROFESSOR WAS SURPRISED WHEN Ms Liu Renfei asked for an appointment. He had begun to think of her as part of his family. But she was entitled to do so and, indeed, was now sitting on the other side of his desk, having arrived precisely at the allotted time.

"I am wondering, professor," she intoned, in a formal manner, "do you think we have souls?"

"Good heavens!" He looked at his watch. "What a question."

Actually, he had wondered about China being Godless. The typical modern state was secular, following the separation of church and state, but the state still paid its respects to God. Think of the Speaker of the House of Representatives in Canberra intoning (without feeling) the Lord's Prayer at the beginning of each day's session. Think of politicians on the stump keen to show how God-fearing they were. The separation of church and state had forced religion out of the world's chancelleries but not from the hearts and minds of the people, and in a democracy it was not wise for a political leader to be different from the people. In China, the state was not only Godless, society was too. Political leaders did not humble themselves before an all-knowing deity. If they were at all inclined to humble themselves, it was at the feet of history or the march of progress or China's destiny, or what the Confucian-Daoists called organic order. If you wished to believe in God, you had to accept a marginal role in society, risk even being seen as cultist.

"I mean," said Renfei, "do you think there is a connection between human rights and religion?"

"No." Having regained his composure, he retraced for his student the history of human rights, showing that it was now, whatever it might have been originally, grounded in equality before the law.

"But," said Renfei, with her puzzled look, "isn't the idea of freedom that something inside each person must be protected? I was wondering whether that might be the soul."

"It might be, for a religious person," he agreed. But for non-believers (including, he remarked, himself), the individual had a public identity, which human rights identified and protected. Being able to vote by secret ballot, not being kept in prison without trial, being able to express an opinion – you did not have to be religious to secure these rights.

Renfei listened carefully. "It wasn't why I came to see you, but I was wondering," she said, offering an explanation for her question. She had discovered Freud. Trying to understand the West's preoccupation with personality, as if something real actually existed inside every person, which for religious people was the soul (not the brain or the mind or the heart), she had come across references to Freudian psycho-analysis. Working backwards from footnotes, she arrived at the man himself. She welcomed Freud at first as a medical scientist who was able to explain this inner person, including its fantasies, by revealing the "unconscious". This Freud was part of the modernist movement, which included Marxism and the Impressionist painters she loved, but after a while she began to worry that Freud's focus on the interior of the person put him in the same camp as religious people.

"His wind is blowing from a different direction, but he finishes up in the same boat," she said. "They all believe there's a self inside that behaves according to its nature." She paused, looking serious, and what the professor had begun to think of as a devil hid behind her eyes.

"I was brought up to believe something different." She smiled diffidently, as if aware of her predicament while not being prepared to apologise for her upbringing.

She was like girls in the Student Christian Movement when he was at university. They were scrubbed and purposeful, and their clothes seemed incidental, even accidental, to their purposes, which required them to be always on the move, rushing from sports and prayer meetings and organising campaigns against the evils of the world. The difference with Renfei was that she was not religious, nor evangelical in the sense of wanting to change everyone. She was a private person, but with an outlook that was purposeful about herself. She was on her way but she kept looking back at you, fearless and imploring at the same time.

Renfei explained that the view she had acquired from parents, teachers and her society was that human beings were connected with their ancestors and with nature. How they behaved depended on how they were brought up and what kind of society they lived in. Everyone had a conscience, which told each person what was right and wrong and how to behave towards other people, but it was not a supra-natural implant. It was the result of human evolution, wisdom acquired over a long period of time and passed on from generation to generation. Right and wrong behaviour in China was pretty much the same as right and wrong according to the Ten Commandments but when Chinese behaved properly, they did so not because they were obeying God or expressing their inner personalities but because everyone knew that was the way to behave.

Ian listened, without offering views of his own. Because of the strange relationship between Mrs Winterbourne and the whirling dervish, he had avoided fashionable theories about relations between children and parents, especially Freudian explanations of repressed sexuality.

Renfei folded her hands. "And now perhaps I can ask you whether you think it is good for society that women speak to the media about breast cancer?"

"What's got into you?" asked the professor, examining his student with mixed amusement and anxiety.

"I never used to think about breast cancer," said Renfei, clear-eyed and with a toss of her head, "but in Australia I have become totally aware of young women who have it, and the suffering they have. I am wondering, if I had breast cancer, how I would behave." She awaited the professor's response and, as none came, continued. "From the point of view of public policy, is it good to worry if you have breast cancer or is it better if you just deal with it if it comes."

She refolded her hands and gave him her "That's what I have been thinking" look.

He understood her problem. The media was full of anguish about young people dying of diseases that were preventible, if medical science were better funded or society were better organised or politicians were not spending their time and taxpayers' money on trips abroad for conferences at which they obviously learned nothing. For the media, the objective was to squeeze every ounce of emotion out of a stricken victim. What good could come of the knowledge that people all over the world were suffering excruciating physical and emotional pain? He made a note for future reference: one of the outcomes of a competitive media was uniformity of response. Each was so anxious not to give rivals an edge that they finished up with almost identical products.

"You're not worried about it, are you?"

"Not really." Renfei meant "a little".

"It's good if you have a friend who can test for symptoms," the professor said. He had read this somewhere, as a corrective to the tendency in young women not to want to discover the truth. And he felt obliged to say that the medical services at universities were good.

"Yes, professor, I know," said Renfei. She giggled. The thought of Lu examining her was so funny.

He sat back, satisfied that he had done all she was asking of him. She straightened her back, throwing off any remnants of despondency, and asked the professor whether, if he were to visit China, he would stop at her university, Tongji, in Shanghai.

"I have been out of mind for my university for so long," she said.

"I understand."

Renfei became coy. She shifted in her seat and looked at him more directly than was necessary. She seemed to be searching for something behind his eyes.

"You should go to Kunming, capital of Yunnan, which has borders with South-East Asia, Vietnam, Laos, Myanmar."

"To pick up some hints on how you are keeping the southern barbarians at bay," said the professor, reclining in an imperial chair.

"Of course." Renfei's mind was elsewhere. "And Yunnan has vistas of pictorial interest. No doubt you have received postcards with pastures of rapeseed?" Receiving no indication whether he had or hadn't, she continued, one hand rolling suggestively in the air. "Yellow fields stretching to the horizon." The other hand moved abruptly upward. "With black hills like pyramids. Greatly picturesque." She was like a tour guide. "The north of China is where government likes to be, but in the south the liveliness of people and nature abound."

She inquired if the professor had thought of visiting Lijiang. "It is not far from Kunming. It is extremely placid." Accustomed to her English, he made no comment. "Lijiang is in a valley with scenery." She might have been reciting from a brochure. "Joseph Rock lived there."

Professor Ferrier nodded understandingly. "Joseph Rock?"

"He came from Europe and taught himself eight languages," said Renfei proudly. The professor agreed that was an achievement, in anyone's language. He allowed himself a self-regarding smile.

"Joseph Rock." Renfei restated the name with an emphatic flip of her tongue, making it sound Chinese. "He lived in Lijiang because of the plants." Her face lit up. "Everything grows in Lijiang. The climate is like Melbourne, only more abundant. It is tropical but also cold, from the mountains." She opened her arms to the sky. "The Tibetan plateau, source of China's great rivers." She intoned, with sweeping hand gestures. "Falling leaves. Trees full of leaves and trees without leaves. Suddenly, leaves everywhere, in the street, on the roof. Just like here. Good for energy in the soil." Her arms twisted upwards. "Also rainforests. Big trees that stop the sun from shining on you. And bamboo. You can eat it, but it is like steel for building."

Excited by the splendid dexterity of the bamboo plant, she examined the professor for a sign he was keeping up with her. "It would be remarkable for you to go to Lijiang."

"I'm sure it would," said Professor Ian Ferrier, endeavouring to look severe, waiting for Ms Liu Renfei to get to the point.

"You could visit Tiger Leaping Gorge," said Renfei hopefully. "Lijiang has many hostels for trekking persons."

The professor wagged his head in disagreement. "I'm not a trekking person." Taking her cue, he thrust an arm down, as if in a bottomless pit. "Especially if Tiger Leaping Gorge is anything like it sounds."

"There are walks and gardens." Ms Liu Renfei twirled and entwined her fingers in the air. "Pleasing for a stroll at evening time." She suddenly remembered. "Lijiang is on the World Heritage List."

The professor decided it was time to be direct. He assumed his benign, inquisitorial face. "May I inquire whether the authorities in Lijiang have engaged Ms Liu to recruit tourists in Australia?"

"It is my home town," said Renfei simply.

"Oh, I didn't know."

"If you visited Lijiang, you could meet my parents." Renfei bit her lip, then burst into tears.

Tearful students, male as well as female, were not a novelty for the professor, but Renfei was a surprise. He had begun to think of her as so sensible and composed, even mature, that an inner life of unresolved emotion had not occurred to him. He moved to comfort her, with a hand on her shoulder. She sniffled into a tissue and then, thanking him with an upward glance, tossed her head to indicate it was over.

Back in the safety of his desk, he cheerfully asked, "So both your parents live in Lijiang?" You could never be sure these days.

Renfei nodded. "They have business. Hostel for backpackers. My father is a doctor."

"How long since you have seen them?"

"More than two years."

She burst again into tears, although this time they were controlled, a recollection of the emotion rather than the feeling itself. Ian Ferrier waited, knowing that the disturbance would pass.

"So you spent your childhood in Lijiang. Lucky you, if it is in a valley with scenery." You adopted Renfei's phrasing after a while.

"It is so beautiful!" Renfei exclaimed, eyes flashing in a tear-stained face. "You would like to shout for joy!"

The professor had not himself ever felt that something was so beautiful that he would like to shout for joy, but he could imagine that the young

Chinese woman sitting opposite him, with flashing eyes and tear-stained face, might have felt that way, might still.

"You had a happy childhood?"

Renfei swayed her body this way and that. "My mum always said that happiness was not something you could have. You might touch it sometimes, but you could never have it."

"Your mother sounds like a wise woman." It occurred to Professor Ferrier that Mrs Winterbourne, on the other hand, might well believe that happiness was something you could put in your pocket and take out when you wanted it. He wondered whether the Chinese had a different idea of happiness from the West. But there were many different views in Western societies. A typically Australian view of happiness was a long weekend away from work, while a typically American attitude was working night and day at something that would make you wealthy.

"She is not always wise, but she never ceases to watch."

"She kept an eye on you."

"When she could." The dutiful daughter was not prepared to have an entirely guiltless childhood.

He paused. He had learned to steer clear of student families. Teaching was difficult enough, getting a huge and complex body of knowledge into a manageable size and shape that would fit into the heads (and hearts and minds) of young men and women. At least, they wanted to learn, and had a lively interest in the market place of ideas and jobs that would determine their future. Families brought something else, practical problems like money or vague and emotional issues that had nothing to do with the classroom, and the most intractable of all, why the student was not valued as highly as the family believed he or she should be.

He comforted himself. Foreign families, being absent, were less of a nuisance. In any case, there was something about Renfei that was different, that touched, even moved him. She was wholesome, meaning not only healthy but uniform, all of one piece. Unlike other girls in the class, she seemed unconcerned about her looks. She wasn't trying to be beautiful, or carefree, or smart or (a couple of conspicuous cases leapt to mind) sexy. On the other hand, she wasn't one of those studious Asian girls, with podgy faces and large-framed glasses, who seemed never to leave childhood, or if they did, with unhappy consequences, and now lounged in their seats, pimply and belligerent. She was a young woman with worldly ambitions who was unusual, it seemed to him, because she gave the impression she was prepared to try to achieve what she wanted on her own. Her personality was already formed, as if she knew who she was in the greater scheme of things.

"Your father? Is he still practising as a doctor?"

"Oh, yes, he keeps going the practice. They are partners in work." She caught the professor's attentive eye. "In China, passion is now in the business."

He knew that when she gave her class presentation, she would be direct and truthful, stating explicitly what she knew and did not know, documenting her material honestly, not using slides and anonymous quotations from the Internet to weave a web of incredible authority for herself. And that was what happened. She grappled head-on with the issue she had chosen, admitting, at the end, that she was only beginning to understand what it was all about.

"Sorry," she said. "I don't think you will leave the class tonight more weightful in your knowledge than before I spoke." But the applause for her was longer than for Jian, who in his presentation had smartly exposed the flaws in the authoritative literature on his chosen subject, using dot points and flow charts and unflattering author photographs and responding to questions with withering replies.

Ian was confident that if he ever did meet her parents, she would not try to take advantage of what would be, after all, merely a simple act of kindness on his part, with no obligations for either of them. He leaned across the desk, assuring Renfei that if he could find a reason to fit Lijiang into the itinerary of his yet undecided trip to China, he would. Of course, he was quick to point out, the matter was not entirely within his competence; the university would provide the funds, requiring him to justify each segment of the journey. But if he did get to Lijiang, he would make a point of meeting her parents.

Ms Liu Renfei's response was unexpected. She stood up abruptly, gave a slight bow in his direction, said "Thank you" in a tone that was neither distant and formal nor personal and intimate, and then on her way out stopped and twirled a couple of delicate steps. Her skirt swirled daintily, as Mrs Winterbourne said it should. He noticed she was dressed differently from class. Pale blue boots came half way up her calves, her elfin costume was shades of mauve and a long cream scarf of silk flowed with her movements. She put her hands in the air and pirouetted to the door, where she paused to beam back a smile.

"Shall we dance, Professor Higgins?" Then she disappeared.

He sat thinking about the surprising Ms Liu. Life's primal forces, which he spent most of his time trying to avoid or, if that were not possible, to keep under control, had found their way to her through some genetic bounty. She had honesty and energy and at the same time she was vulnerable in a way that women normally were not. She offered herself with a lightness and openness that was almost insupportable.

He wondered if this could be the passionate young voice of the new China, hidden from the public, including himself, by an overlay of old concepts like power and interests, and old precepts like realism and prudence. Perhaps her generation would startle the world with their freshness.

Her reference to Professor Higgins was intriguing. She had probably seen the film *My Fair Lady*, which she might not have known was based on George Bernard Shaw's play *Pygmalion*, itself based on the Greek myth of the statue Galatea coming to life to fulfil the desire of Pygmalion, king of Cyprus. Perhaps she wanted to show off the elfin costume or the blue boots. Women liked to display themselves. She was surely not trying to make the point that he was a Pygmalion, wanting to reshape her according to his idea of what a young woman from China should be like. Well, he wasn't. He didn't even bother to correct her grammar.

He smiled to himself. She would be surprised to learn that he enjoyed dancing. He had a bit of the whirling dervish in him. He had been too young for the big bands, but there was a time, when he was courting a psychiatrist's daughter, when white-tie balls were still flaunted in the face of counter-cultural love-ins; they had glided together as if they were fated to spend life in each other's arms. He could show Ms Liu Renfei a thing or two on the dance floor. The body, under aesthetic discipline, had its place in the pantheon of life's splendours.

Professor Ferrier paused. To guard against the possibility (remote, yet not negligible) that some people might believe he was tempted to "do something" with Ms Liu Renfei, he would need to protect their relationship with the rigours of scholarship. She and her parents (and perhaps her grandparents?) would be his case study of the new China. It would have the advantage of freshness, demographically apt but, with real people, unconstrained by models, paradigms and variables. He sat back, pleased with his conceptual ingenuity, and then was almost immediately afflicted with doubt. Was this taking advantage of her in a way that framers of university regulations, trapped in popular perceptions of what was proper and improper, seemed not to have foreseen? Was this abuse of the power inherent in the relationship of teacher with student? Was this treating Renfei and her family like specimens under the microscope on the dissecting table?

Professor Ferrier did a Renfei. He collapsed in his chair with his hands in the air. He then realised that they had met with the door closed, contrary to his rule that his office should be open when female students were present.

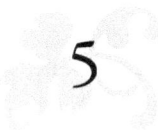

5

RENFEI THREADED HER WAY THROUGH the fronds and tendrils of the secret garden and turned the key in the lock of the door with panels of stained glass. She entered, inhaling the familiar smell of wood and woollen carpets, and half turned to take the corridor to Mr Winterbourne's office, when from the corner of one eye she saw him sitting in a large grandfather chair of woven rattan, with a high formal back and winged rosewood arms, that he had bought in Singapore half a century ago.

He was dressed to receive visitors, which meant that a tartan scarf of dominant red was thrown over the shoulder of his navy blue jacket. He rose to his feet and waved her to a waiting chair.

"I have been examining some photographs of Duke Kahanamoku, the young Hawaiian who introduced board surfing to Australia in 1914," he said. "He was the original big kahuna!"

As Renfei did not get the allusion, he changed tack. "The extraordinary thing is that the first Australian to ride a board was a Sydney schoolgirl, Isabel Letham." Renfei beamed her pleasure as receipt of the information.

"The point is this," said the guru curtly. He raised his nose and sniffed, as if compelled to consider something distasteful. "Australia's identity is bound up with being British and the British came across the Indian Ocean." He spoke against the grain, in pursuit of truth, and bunched his shoulders to take the strain. "Don't be misled by Captain Cook and the transit of Venus, Tahiti, Hawaii and all that carry on." He watched her anxiously while his awkward intelligence sank in. "The imperial lifeline, the red thread of honour, connected Australia with the homeland through the Suez Canal, like the rest of the empire."

He peered at her. "Posh." He spelled it out, watching her carefully. "Port out, PO, starboard home, SH. Posh." He examined her eyes. "The sun on the right side. Got it?"

Renfei nodded, after a long hesitation. "Posh," she said wonderingly.

"The Panama Canal! Who cared? The Pacific was full of foreigners – Spanish, Portuguese, Dutch, French, German, American, north and south, then Japanese and Chinese." He was watching her closely. "You follow?"

She nodded, but with slow, exaggerated movements to suggest she needed more time.

"New Zealand has settled down where it is. It has become a Pacific island. But Australia?" He stood up for emphasis. "Australia would like to be in the northern hemisphere with the big countries."

Seated, he inquired, "You have read the book written by the esteemed professor?"

Renfei laughed. "We have to."

The guru was on his feet again, stalking his prey. "He looks to the northern hemisphere, where all the powerful nations are, the US, Europe, India, China, Japan. He wants to work out how Australians can fit into the picture of the world they have created." An aerial finger raised a possibility. "How, perhaps, Australia can itself become powerful?" But that prospect had never matured. "As Charles Darwin said when he was leaving Australia: 'Too great for affection, not great enough for respect.'"

Mr Winterbourne looked intently at Renfei, as if gauging how much she could take. "If you look at the Pacific, there is no power or combination of powers. There is just space. No military might, no industrial or commercial influence, no political authority, no cultural signature. Powerless." He smiled with the wisdom of far-off things, and resumed his seat. "Like the Aborigines. Powerless."

Ms Liu Renfei considered the plight of the Australian Aborigines with her head suitably bowed.

"Bloody marvellous!" said the guru. "Available to predators and benefactors alike. Australia has a choice. We can be predator or benefactor." She could see that he wished what he was saying to be taken seriously, and waited. "Of course, you will say, we wish to be benefactor. But if we wish to be benefactor we have to know who we are and what we want to give them. It is a big question. Who are we and what do we want to give them?" He rolled his eyes at the enormity of the challenge.

Mr Winterbourne was saying what her father used to say. But the guru had reached a decisive moment. He stood suddenly, strode to a wall of bookshelves and took out an atlas. He rearranged their chairs and spread the atlas on his knee, inviting her to lean over.

"The Pacific Ocean. This happened. That happened." He searched her face for confirmation of what he was about to say. "History is on the surface, quick." He fluttered his hands. "Geography is underneath, slow." His hands unfolded in slow circles.

"I was wondering," Renfei said courteously, yet intending to stem the flow, "if I could visit the Pacific Ocean while I am on my voyage to Australia."

He examined the map, turning it sideways. "You would have to cross the border." His voice became low and cautious. Crossing the border from Victoria into New South Wales was a serious undertaking.

He leaned back to survey his guest from top to toe. "There's the black dolphin," he said solemnly.

Renfei was excited. "I love the way they jump at the water, in and out."

"A motel," said the guru. "The Black Dolphin in Merimbula." He explained that once upon a time it was popular with romantic couples from Melbourne. Renfei supposed, from the aura of contentment that suddenly surrounded Mr Winterbourne, that he was speaking from personal experience.

"In those days, it was overnight, on your way to Sydney." He weighed in his mind how much this young woman from China needed to know about Australia in the days of his youth. "Escape across the border. Warm waters of the Pacific. Drive in. Modern motel. No questions asked."

"It sounds like a welcome place," said Renfei.

"A friend of mine built it," said the guru, with a touch of pride. "He was a modern architect. Before architects became post-modern."

Renfei nodded. "Post-modern is very old-fashioned."

The guru enjoyed that. He slapped a hand on one thigh, and then both hands on both thighs. He became immersed in distant thoughts, from the depths of which he suddenly aroused himself, blinking in the morning light. He stood, moving nimbly in the direction of the drawing room, announcing over his shoulder, "I have a surprise for you."

Parked at the back of the house was a small red car, shining in the sun.

"How would you like that?" he asked.

One of Renfei's dreams was to get a driver's licence in Australia so that she could drive a car, the symbol in China of freedom and modernity. One day, when she was a successful professional woman in China and had repaid her parents for her costly education in Australia, she might even own a little car like this one.

"I am overpowered by it."

"It's not a stretch limo," said Mr Winterbourne, twisting his lips to show he knew he was being humorous. "Mrs Winterbourne ..." He paused to arrange his thoughts. "When she was a chick." He wiggled his body in remembrance of Mrs Winterbourne's chicken days.

"It has a cute nose, like a puppy dog's," Renfei said.

Mr Winterbourne nodded gravely. "It's yours if you want it."

Renfei's confusion moved into higher gear. She smiled stupidly, wondering if her understanding of English were faulty.

"Mrs Winterbourne ..." her host repeated, as if that might explain everything. Renfei acknowledged with a nod the mutually agreed wonder of Mrs Winterbourne.

"Well, there it is." He held out a bundle of keys. "Take it. I'll fix up the paperwork."

Renfei twisted on her heels, declining the proffered keys. An adolescent pout appeared, proclaiming the injustice of the world. "I'm only a student. I can't afford ..."

"Nothing to pay," Mr Winterbourne interrupted, airily waving a hand. "She had it for ages." He lowered his eyes. "Like a flapper." He assumed a solemn appearance. "Now she's a mature woman. Get another one."

"I don't possess a licence which would give me the authority to drive a car," said Renfei, finding a patch of ground on which she could stand in a swirling universe.

"Oh." The guru was jolted by this unexpected obstacle in the way of his brilliant surprise. He had assumed that these days all young women could drive cars. He quickly recovered. "We'll soon fix that. Get you into one of those driving schools." He stood back to scrutinise her from head to toe, evaluating her fitness. "Do it on your ear."

Giving the car to Renfei took a weight off the guru's mind. It was taking up space in the garage and she was a likeable young woman from a Pacific neighbour whose parents weren't able to buy a car for her, as some of the rich Hong Kong families did for their kids in Australia. So bingo! He was confident she would handle the whole thing sensibly.

"I like the look of her," he said to Mrs Winterbourne, as if evaluating a horse or a yacht.

Veronica had been his favourite daughter, which was why he hadn't trusted his emotions when he gave the car to Renfei saying it was Mrs Winterbourne's. His other daughter, Gillian (with a soft "g" and never shortened to Gilly), was the trial of his life. She was prolific in whatever she did, producing wealth, social photo opportunities and grandchildren at a pace he sometimes thought was not humanly acceptable. She and her husband had a successful partnership in Melbourne, a combination of media interests, especially commercial television (she had her own show), an art gallery and a chain of women's fashion outlets. Her success had given her an "iconic" (meaning irrational) position of authority in the media, which she had transformed into a position of authority in general, especially in relation to him.

She had decided that Charlie Boy needed to straighten up. It seemed to him and Mrs Winterbourne that every spare minute of her time (admittedly not many) was spent on devising ways in which he could be straightened up and every other spare minute was spent in transferring this information by telephone to the house in Queens Road. "You need to pay attention to your shirts," she might say. "Stripes are in. But not for ties. Plain ties for striped shirts." And: "Living in that ramshackle place is not a good look. You should move to Docklands. That's where the wheelers and dealers are." Or: "All that jolly boatman stuff is a bit old hat. Why don't you get yourself on a couple of decent boards?"

Gillian had the knack of being charming in public and obnoxious in private. She was revered by masses as the pretty blonde woman on television with the lovely smile. Even those close to her at work shared the public's perception because she was on her best behaviour not only before the cameras but also whenever she occupied public space. To her nearest and dearest, on the other hand (or the other side of the front door), she was nasty.

"I don't know why she keeps having children," said Mrs Winterbourne, "when she obviously doesn't like them."

"Oh, I wouldn't go that far." The jolly boatman had decided long ago to look on the bright side. At least she wasn't after what little money he had left.

"She's highly strung," he offered.

"Highly strung!" Mrs Winterbourne's scorn was volcanic. "She's a bitch."

Charlie Boy wasn't sure what Mrs Winterbourne meant by being a bitch. Well, at least Gillian couldn't be called a slut. He was careful of the reputation of the girls' mother, as it was presumably from her that bitchiness, whatever it was, had descended. His first wife had been a darling, a good-looker with a swinging stride that had forced her skirt against her thighs in the most enticing manner. She wore captivating hats, snug little ear-huggers and huge things in summer that took off like kites in a breeze. She had a wonderful personality, free and easy, happy-go-lucky, devil may care, whatever. Indeed, that was her typical response. "Whatever!" With her hands in the air. The photographer chap she had run off with to Paris was a lapse in judgment, but he didn't blame her, although dumping the girls on him was a bit much. But we all do silly things, don't we? And Gillian, for all her pushing and shoving, had achieved a lot. Still, he wished she would leave him alone. He wasn't hurting anyone.

So it was that Renfei, who was barely able to pay the rent she shared with Lu for a one-bedroom flat in East St Kilda and worked as cleaning lady for Mrs Winterbourne to help pay her living expenses, took driving lessons, passed the test and became the owner of a natty little red car, the envy of her fellow students, which she could not afford to run and for which there was no parking space in her block of flats. Parked in the street, with a local resident's permit, she worried that someone would steal it.

"I need more money," she told Lu.

"There's money to be made," said Lu, "if you put your mind to it."

"How?"

"The lottery. And the casino."

No true Chinese would deny the destiny of numbers and the authority of chance, but she needed a small, steady increment, not the flickering hope of a win.

"I mean money in my hand."

"You can take off your clothes in clubs."

"Don't be silly."

"You can earn a lot of money. Cash. They poke it at you."

"What do you mean – poke?"

"They fold the money and poke it into your panties."

"How can they, if I am taking them off?"

They giggled themselves into silence, hands over mouths.

Then Professor Ferrier announced to his class that he was intending to visit China and wished to appoint someone with Chinese language skills to help him, translating journal articles and assisting him with his itinerary. The job would need to be officially advertised by the university's central administration, but as there were several Chinese students in his class who might be interested, he thought he could – without breaking the rules – let them know personally. The work would attract the required university rate per hour (which he did not know and disdained by twisting his lips to disparage the implications of "attract") and would be deliberately kept under 20 hours a week (to allow foreign students on temporary visas to apply).

"It won't make you rich, but it will help to pay the rent," he told the class.

"And run a car," said Renfei to herself. She applied and was not really surprised when she got the job.

"Teacher's pet," said Lu, masking her delight.

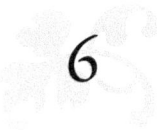

6

"Would you like a spin in my little red car? I am proposing a journey to the Dandenong Ranges for Sunday afternoon tea at The Old Curiosity Shop, which has been discovered from your mother, the esteemed Mrs Winterbourne."

It was seemly enough, but when the professor received Ms Liu Renfei's e-mail his built-in alarm detector rang a couple of bells. What if they were seen by someone from the university, tootling about in her little red car on a Sunday, or worse, in a pas de deux in some Dandenong glade or, secluded by aspidistras, at The Old Curiosity Shop?

"Will your friend Lu be coming?" he asked, leaving her to guess why he thought it necessary to ask.

"I was thinking of riding tandem," replied the ebullient Ms Liu.

The professor expressed the opinion, leaving open the question whether or not he was accepting, that it would be more appropriate to use his car, with himself as driver and provider of refreshments at The Old Curiosity Shop, on the grounds that Ms Liu was a guest in his country and he was probably more acquainted with the twists and turns on the narrow mountain roads than she could be, careful and well advised by the redoubtable Mrs Winterbourne as she undoubtedly was.

Whether or not Renfei disentangled his syntax, she remained determined. "I am a small person in a strange land and I wish to offer retribution for your bounty," she replied.

Oh, well. He sent off a laborious acceptance, in which he made play of their research together and the opportunity this would provide for further investigation into the important matters that they needed to follow up, using as much academic jargon as he could. A cursory reader of the e-mails might have thought he was helping her to complete an application for a job at the World Bank.

So, on Sunday morning, she waited in the little red car at the appointed time outside his building and when he appeared, opened the door on the passenger's side and stood by, as if to attention.

"Good morning," said the professor, dressed, as Lu would have noted, in various folds of pastel-coloured warm clothing, which required him to squeeze himself rather precisely into the space allotted to the front seat passenger in the little car.

Side on, she was a delightful companion, face glowing, eyes darting, hair freshly washed, flying, not tousled. She drove as if the vehicle were a personal appendage, leaning forward, swaying to one side and the other in harmony with her steering, keeping all three rear-vision mirrors in view, juggling the taped music, chatting to her illustrious passenger, extolling the virtues of the little red vehicle.

"She's quite nippy." (A Winterbourneism, surely.) "I am calling her Vivien. Would you agree that's a nippy name?"

"I would." Did she know whose car it had really been? You never knew with Charlie Boy. He might have told her.

"I am pleased to be ascending mountains," said Renfei. "Life in Melbourne has been very stable." She glanced at the recumbent professor. After a nervous start, he had reclined into a drowsy acceptance of the car and its driver, seemingly connected by invisible tissues. "Life is really a mountain trail, isn't it?"

Professor Ferrier stirred himself. "I trust you don't have trailblazing in mind today."

"No," said Renfei. "I am in a state of sedation."

"The Old Curiosity Shop is about as sedate as you can get, while still remaining upright," said the professor.

Renfei chuckled. "Everyone in class is happy when you make jokes."

The professor accepted the compliment gracefully. One of maturity's assets was a capacity to receive, as well as to give. You had reached a sustainable balance in which either side could be topped up from time to time without detriment to the other. He decided to use the opportunity to inquire more deeply into his young driver's future.

"So, what are you proposing to do when you finish the course?"

Renfei was pensive. "I have to untangle my thoughts."

"You don't know?"

"I am traversing prospects."

"But don't you have some idea of the kind of job you might apply for? I mean, government, business, one of those NGOs. The United Nations?"

Renfei turned fully in his direction and he could see the trouble in her eyes.

"Do you think my parents could live in Australia?"

The professor did not fully understand the system by which students from abroad were awarded points for courses, depending on the immigration authorities' judgment of whether one course of study was more relevant to Australia's needs than another. A certain total of points would give the student the right to apply for a working visa and then, after a period of employment, for permanent residency. All he knew was that accountancy had a high ranking, with the consequence that many students took accountancy courses without any of the appropriate skills, like a facility with mathematics, and failed. And the authorities kept changing the points, moving the goal posts.

"Why would they want to do that? Pay a visit, perhaps. But why live here?"

"They have been working so hard," said Renfei. He noticed a trembling lower lip and put out a hand to touch her, then withdrew it, not knowing where to place it. He could see a smooth, round knee.

"I understand."

They drove in silence, as the road rose imperceptibly on a long, straight incline through industrial estates before entering the foothills, where it wound through sudden forests of tall, slender trees, ferns and brush, hidden houses with only an iron roof, painted red or green, to show that people lived there, perched seemingly amid branches, like tree houses. He thought of the hill stations of India which he knew not from ever having been there but from boyhood reading of Rudyard Kipling, Somerset Maugham and other chroniclers of the collision of the British Empire with the human heart. The early Australian settlers did what the British imperialists did, escaping the heat of the plains in summer not by sprawling on beaches but by gaining the cool air of height and hiding themselves in greenery.

But the experience of the human heart in the greenery of the Dandenongs had been left to fate. The early chroniclers were busy with bird calls and strange animals, the lure of land to farm and gold to mine and the promise of not having to doff the cap. He glanced across at Renfei's profile, which was eagerly absorbing the landscape. Would a young Chinese woman driving her little red car up this ascent, taking in everything for the first time, leave an emotional trace or just disappear into the mountain air, like all the others?

Now they were in Tudor England, thatched cottages with white-daubed walls cross-stitched in blackened wood. Also, summoned by Renfei's shriek of recognition, the England of Charles Dickens! Her cry of excitement, as if she had personally discovered Ye Olde Curiosity Shoppe (as it became in a stencilled board across the front), may also have been because it lived up to her expectations. It stood alone, right on the street, a rickety wooden cottage without porch or veranda, with a narrow front and seemingly endless extensions at the rear. It was as singular a place as you could hope to find on a Sunday jaunt undertaken without any idea of what was in store.

She pulled the little red car over into a parking area and consulted some notes she had made on Mrs Winterbourne's mauve notepaper. "Would you like a Devonshire afternoon tea?"

The professor was not partial to Devonshire teas. They represented an Australian past that was both boring and unhealthy for middle-aged men keen to stay trim. He glanced unnecessarily at his watch and remarked that it was still morning, which ruled out the possibility of afternoon tea. He begged to add that the lashings of cream and jam that the Devonshire label in mountain retreats unfailingly provided, as if the ascent both enlarged people's appetite and deprived them of their senses, were not his cup of tea.

His humour did not reach Renfei, who was examining the mauve notepaper. "Should we proceed to the tower at One Tree Hill?"

"We have already passed One Tree Hill," said the professor in a dismissive tone that made it seem unworthy of a visit.

"The lookout on Mount Dandenong?" Renfei sounded apprehensive, as if her faith in the esteemed Mrs Winterbourne was fading.

"Let's have a walk," said Ian, surprising himself with his vigour as he was already outside the car. He had noticed a gully of enticing green winding around a hill that, if it were not fenced off, would make a nice vantage point from which to assess the world at the end of a ten-minute encounter with nature.

She took his arm. It was a strange sensation to have a woman on his arm. It had never happened before. None of the women he had known had been in the habit of taking men's arms. They were inclined to stride ahead. If they did take anything it would be a hand, swung between walkers as a symbol of equality. Mrs Winterbourne, who was known to favour walking in parks (she prevailed upon Dr Charles Winterbourne, AM, to write to the appropriate authorities about the obtrusion of tree roots on pathways) did not take arms or swing hands. So he had not expected Renfei to take his arm. He had thought she would skip and bounce at his side, asking obvious or imponderable questions, tangling with undergrowth, scrambling up slopes.

But Ms Liu Renfei definitely took the arm of Professor Ian Ferrier, who did not try to dislodge her. He liked both the idea and the sensation. He could feel the warmth of her body through the cladding of their jackets. He also felt something else, something intellectual, even perhaps emotional, a feeling of setting out together, a venture, perhaps an adventure. He was tempted to squeeze her arm to show his appreciation, which he did. She squeezed back and looked up at him with a smile of friendship.

They tottered and slid together in a tiny remnant of primeval Australia, boarding its murmuring waters on old, slippery stones, skirting logs that might have fallen in another era and were decomposing so slowly that they still obstructed impudent intruders from the plains. Was this what people meant by having "fun". He could not recall the last time he had experienced, or even been near, fun.

"Look!" Renfei had seen a flash of colour against the green of the undergrowth and the blue of the sky. "Is that a lyrebird?"

Lu had prepared her by describing her Jewish boyfriend's first visit to the Dandenongs. On a family excursion, he had seen a lyrebird, with its fabled tail of peacock colours ("but more delicate, twitching and swishing"). It was rare to see a lyrebird and some people said if you saw one on your first visit you were being offered a gift which you would never be able to replay for the rest of your life ("or something like that").

Ian followed Renfei's pointing finger but saw nothing. He was sceptical; lyrebirds lived in dense thickets of forest, not in fingers of green on pastoral land. "Perhaps a king parrot?" His mind was set on the hill. He wanted to stand on it, arm in arm with Renfei, in possession of all they surveyed.

And they did. The post-and-wire fence was easily breached. They stood together on top of the hill and surveyed the landscape. She disentangled her arm and strode about, scanning the horizon. At their back were the ranges, the flickering end of the Great Dividing Range, a barrier that ran all the way down the east of Australia, dividing coastal civilisation from the promise of arable land on the other side and inhospitable stretches in the vast beyond, inhabited by people of another world. Before them was a sloping plain, shimmering with silent movement and flickering light, and in the distance the city, rising on the horizon like an outcrop of phantom flora in a desert.

She swept the horizon with her disengaged arm. "It has scenery, like Lijiang."

She stood erect, but her shoulders slumped and he noticed she brushed a tear from her cheek. He took a quick, single step and, suddenly, she turned and was in his arms. He could feel her body, especially the fullness of her breasts. He patted her shining head of hair.

"Let's have Devonshire morning tea. Or apple tart, blueberry muffins or whatever you fancy."

Renfei disentangled herself. "You are in a mood of gluttony," she said approvingly, accepting his arm again.

Ye Olde Curiosity Shoppe was devoted to warmth and conviviality. A beaming male attendant with rosy cheeks escorted them through the rickety building to a small room lined with wooden cupboards containing antique crockery, where they were given a table for two near a log fire. A beaming waitress with blonde curls stood by while they scanned a voluminous menu in scrolled lettering. It was now approaching legitimate lunchtime and he chose toasted sandwiches. She, loyal to the Winterbournes, selected something with the Devonshire label, rolling her eyes and patting her stomach in doleful anticipation. They shared a two-cup teapot.

Then, eye to eye, they asked each other the kinds of questions they had not asked before.

"Have you been married, professor?" She inquired with kindly concern, as if worrying whether he had ever suffered from a serious illness. She hesitated, unsure if she had the right tense. "Ever?"

"No, never." He got that out of the way quickly.

"And the temptation never came over you?"

"It crossed my mind, but it never seemed to cross the mind of anyone else at the same time." His flippant response was meant to put an end to this line of questioning, which it did, although a supplementary question was enticing Renfei.

"If Australian and Chinese people marry, is the result better than either or worse than both?" She grimaced. "Or neither?"

"What a question!" said the professor. "You're really something."

"You mean really someone, don't you, professor?"

"I mean something, in the sense of ... off the page."

"What does it mean ... off the page?"

"It means beyond the bounds of reason." He examined his student with a touch of impatience. "It's obvious, isn't it? It depends on who the individuals are, not whether they are Chinese and Australian."

"I was thinking of Chinese good features," said Renfei. "And bad ones."

"Which are?"

She put her hand over her mouth. "Slit eyes and squashed noses."

"Mrs Winterbourne thinks Chinese women are the most perfectly formed female species in the entire world," said the professor.

"Really." Renfei was impressed. "Mrs Winterbourne has tasteful opinions." She contemplated her hands. "It is true our ears are not large and our chins do not stick out. Also, of course, we are not prone to making freckles. Although in some English novels freckles are ..." She searched his face for the precise word.

"Fetching?" he suggested.

The professor decided to make a sweeping statement. He normally avoided sweeping statements, which were designed to draw attention to the wit or imagination of their authors rather than to the truth or authenticity of their content.

"If you and I were to marry, the war of the worlds would be nothing compared with the collision of our genes."

The words were barely out of his mouth when he regretted them. He should never make sweeping statements. Renfei showed her disapproval by lowering her head and failing to raise her voice in response.

"You are having me for fun," she said gravely. "Actually, if our good features were doubled, the result could be enhancing."

"Tell me my good features," said the professor, reduced to cunning.

"Your eyes are kind. And I am grateful for the way your hair turns back from your forehead."

Charmed, he returned her compliment the only way he knew. "And you are trustworthy. I cannot think of a more enhancing attribute than that."

It was true. She was the first woman in his adult life he felt he could trust. He wondered how it had happened and what were its implications. They were both silent, aware that a point in the conversation had been reached where it might be difficult to resume the banter.

"Do you have a boyfriend?" the professor asked abruptly.

"Only in China," she said, as if that, taking into account the distance she had travelled to be the professor's student in Melbourne (and the warmth of a small back room at Ye Olde Curiosity Shoppe), did not count.

"A Lijiang boy?" He could see her on her way home from school, frolicking in fields of yellow rapeseed perforated by limestone tops in a scenic valley.

"Not really." Renfei's temporising smile might have meant yes, but could have meant no. "We met at university in Shanghai."

"You mean, he was from Lijiang, but you didn't meet until university in Shanghai?"

Ms Liu seemed to be considering a delicate issue. Her body swayed, she nibbled carefully at the outskirts of a large cream-encrusted scone, then took a deep draught of tea from a willow-patterned cup, which might have come from one of the wooden cupboards.

"Yes, at Tongji university."

"But not from Lijiang?" He was demolishing the toasted sandwiches, but was determined to establish a point in the conversation that she seemed inclined to avoid.

Renfei nodded. "Yes, he is from Lijiang."

And it emerged that Sunday afternoon in the cluttered, back room of Ye Olde Curiosity Shoppe in the Dandenong Ranges, a little more than an hour's drive from Melbourne, that the boyfriend of Ms Liu Renfei had disappeared. It was a piece of her life she had told no one, not even Lu. Certainly not her parents.

The boy was from Lijiang, but had been at school in Kunming, so they had not met until they arrived, by different routes, at Tongji university.

"We were sick for home and we would be together for hours just talking about Lijiang," Renfei said. "People from Shanghai would go there to celebrate some family occasion and they would come back talking about it. Lijiang is so beautiful, they would say. And we would just sit there, thinking about Lijiang to ourselves."

He became a student leader. He took her one night to a meeting, but she did not like the people.

"They were not only students. They were men from outside, and some of them were rough. There was one man older than the others who was quiet all the time but looked as if he knew everything. People seemed unsure about him, wanting his opinion, but not asking."

Not long after this meeting, there was a crackdown on student activity at Tongji and her boyfriend was taken away. She tried to find him, but no one would tell her where he was, or what had happened. She stood in queues, sat in the waiting rooms of police stations.

"Was he charged with anything or just detained?" the professor inquired.

Renfei was not sure. She asked: "What has he done?" They answered: "If he has done something wrong, he will know what it is." "Who are you?" they demanded, as if she had no right to be asking. "What do you want? Show me your identity card. Go back to your class."

Then she was told that her application to go to Australia had been successful. Her parents were pleased. She had not told them about him. So she left for Australia and had heard nothing about him since. She had no idea where he was.

"Does he have a name?" asked Professor Ian Ferrier.

"I have been unable to utter his name," said Renfei. "I thought it might be bad luck, if someone heard it."

"It doesn't matter. But it must bother you, not knowing where he is."

"He is probably back at Tongji." Ms Renfei Liu resumed something of her old buoyancy. "Since I came to Australia, I have been lost in my studies. That was why I thought, when you were there ..." She was thoughtful. "In China, so many people are coming and going that no one knows where they are."

"So you have lost him. Or he has lost you."

The professor decided to put an end to the boyfriend's existence. The young lady sitting opposite him was a delightful prospect, not just for some young man lost in China but for the world at large, which included him. "What's next on our agenda?"

Renfei consulted Mrs Winterbourne's mauve notepaper. She decided they must go to Rickett's Sanctuary, where the Aboriginal people had been "made into trees". As they were leaving, after he had paid and tipped the beaming waitress, Renfei's quick eye caught something. "Look!" She pointed over her shoulder. At a corner table were two heads close together, Matthew Burnside and Verya Morewitz, son of Johnno and daughter of Marty, too engrossed in themselves to notice anyone else. "Shall we accost them?"

Professor Ian Ferrier became his father's son, whisking her from the dance floor in a single movement. "They're heading for marriage," he muttered, as if they might be contagious.

"You are respecting their privacy?" Renfei inquired breathlessly, as they piled into the little red car. The professor was silent. "Or perhaps you do not want them to see us?"

She busied herself with the ignition key. He was wondering whether his mother might have plotted the whole thing.

"Why should I not want them to see us?" His injured look was unconvincing and Renfei engaged the gear.

"She is quite beautiful. I envy her European profile," she said, changing the subject. "You have been to Europe, professor?" He had, and was pleased to expand on the "idea" of Europe and the principle of "subsidiarity" underlying the new Europe until they reached Rickett's Sanctuary.

They also visited Mount Dandenong and a nursery in Olinda that Charlie Boy liked, and the little red car even found a way back to One Tree Hill. The boyfriend and the lovers were not mentioned again and Renfei was her usual self, wholesome and cheerful.

As they descended into the real world of sprawling Melbourne, with Renfei extolling the virtues of the Winterbourne family and the little red car, the professor decided to tell her about Veronica. He had been examining his motives all afternoon. His detachment from family had been jolted by the way Renfei seemed effortlessly to have become fond of both his mother and stepfather. Was he jealous? He brushed the suspicion aside in the interests of intellectual integrity. She should know.

So he told Renfei that the little red car had belonged to Charlie Boy's younger daughter, who had one day driven it to an isolated spot on the Mornington Peninsula and killed herself.

7

THE VICE-CHANCELLOR WAS TIRED. HE explained to Professor Ferrier that he was preparing the budget, which was always exhausting. The Australian dollar was like a yoyo and when you depended on overseas students for a healthy slice of revenue, the value of the Aussie was crucial. But was it an independent or dependent variable? That was the question. He wondered aloud whether being a vice-chancellor was like being asked to drink from a poisoned chalice.

Then he looked intently at the professor. "There've been some reports about your classes, Ian," he said.

"Reports?"

"Not the actual classes." The vice-chancellor seemed to be choosing his words carefully. "The library."

"The library?"

"We've been asked to keep an eye on anything unusual on inter-library loans."

"Unusual?"

"Technical. Bomb-making, that sort of thing. And inflammatory stuff."

"I thought you got all that on the Web."

"You can, apparently, but we've got to keep our eyes open in our own neck of the woods," said the vice. Campus security was his responsibility but there was always a danger that something would happen in class, he explained. Students had tense and emotional lives. Mostly, after failed affairs and disappointing academic results, they let off steam outside the classroom, but if the source of the tension was within class, and depended on how sensitive topics were handled, they might be tempted to express their frustration in class.

"So, there's a good chap, Ian. Keep an eye on it."

That seemed to be the end of the interview and Ian wondered why the vice-chancellor had bothered. Covering his back, no doubt. If anything did happen, there was a record of a meeting in which Professor Ferrier had been told to tighten up security. Without any indication of what needed to be done or any offers of support from the central administration. Typical.

But the vice-chancellor was not finished.

"You'd be surprised, Ian, if you knew what's going on. Here we are, engaged in what you might reasonably think is among the more uplifting of human endeavours, education, and there are people who can't wait to get their grubby fingers into it."

He scowled, his face clouded and he leaned forward confidentially.

"I hope you will be surprised to learn, Ian, that there are people in this town, lawfully accredited people, whose speciality is falsifying students' examination marks in their country of origin so they qualify for education here, and when they are here, continuing the practice."

"But how?" The professor, puzzled by the vice-chancellor's extra-curriculum excursion, was on firm ground at last. He had served on numberless examination boards in which marks were suspiciously checked and double-checked. Too many "high distinctions" or "fails" created a distortion of the ideal marking pattern that had to be explained.

"You would be surprised, Ian," said the vice, shaking his head. After some thought, he decided to be only slightly more informative. "Between biro and paper on examination day and the results later on the Web, there are opportunities for skulduggery." He sighed. "As T.S. Eliot remarked, between the idea and the reality falls the shadow."

Having introduced poetry into the conversation, he became more expansive.

"The system is now so big and overloaded there is scope for manipulation." His smile was murky. "For adding value, you might say." He leaned back in his chair and examined the professor, assessing his level of empathy. "Think of the furore in the media about art and pornography. A painting of a young woman, beautiful in its naked tenderness, or should I more accurately say, tender nakedness, is displayed in a gallery to expert acclaim and aesthetic appreciation. Then postcards of the painting are commercially sold, to anyone, including those who make a living retailing them in dark streets. And, as part of a marketing strategy, the postcard is posted on the Web, where it becomes the noisome property of a paedophile ring.

"Different realities." He seemed to think his point had been sufficiently made.

"The age of enlightenment, Ian, is yet to dawn." He allowed his shoulders to slump. "I am sometimes compelled to believe that the entire world is engaged in transactions that are either illicit or immoral." He scowled again, then softened as he prepared a conclusive sentence. "We teach our students about the authority of reason and as soon as they get out of the classroom they are seduced by misfits and scoundrels whose sole objective in life, you might be forgiven for thinking, is to make money by evading the law or misleading or mistreating their fellow men. Or women."

Were he not flustered by budget anxieties and overwhelmed with indignities and misdemeanours, the vice-chancellor would have presented a trim, pleasing appearance. He had been a snappy dresser and useful tennis player in his youth. A medical man, he had moved to academia attracted by opportunities for research but by serial contingencies, for which he was totally unprepared (including the discovery that a predecessor had his fingers in the till), he had been catapulted into high administrative office. Concerned that it might be thought that he had forsaken his calling, he embarked on an ambitious campaign to legalise the use of social drugs. His arguments were impeccable: prohibition did not work; removing criminality would undermine the drug culture that it fostered; young people should learn that liberty was a responsibility, not just a right. But the churches, the media and the politicians would have none of it. Nor would the public.

Friends on the university council had drawn him aside and told him that unless he dropped his campaign the "powers that be" would move against him. In other words, he was told to pull his head in. He took their advice. Society had a deep-seated aversion to any measure that allowed individuals to decide how they might live or die, he decided, even when it could be shown that the measure was itself beneficial. Since then, he had been troubled by spasms of paranoia, which showed in a nervous, peevish manner.

"But falsifying marks?"

It was like clinging to a grain of sand, but Ian was dogged. At moments like these, he reminded himself that he had written a small, useful book, while everyone was quarrelling about what kind of big book should be written.

"There's many a slip, twixt the cup and the lip," said the vice-chancellor with a sniff. He shuffled papers on his desk, bit his lip, looked towards the door as if he were expecting someone, then reached out to a folder and tossed it across the desk.

"Minutes of the last council meeting. Have a look at it later. People are getting edgy. I need someone to give me a hand."

Ian idly thumbed through the minutes, marking time.

"The trouble is," said the vice-chancellor mournfully, "that if a sub-committee of council is set up to monitor campus security, or if someone is officially appointed, you draw attention to the problem, bring it into the open. You might think that is a good thing, which it is in the abstract, but in real life, if I may presume to use such a phrase, it provides those who are interested in evading security with an incentive." He surveyed the professor, seemingly from a height. "You see my point?" He decided, in any case, to explain it. "If there's a structure, they will work out ways of getting around it. If they don't know we're on the lookout, they might be caught unawares."

Ian nodded in a manner intended to suggest agreement, with reservations yet unspoken.

"It's the old story," said the bureaucratic warrior. "As soon as you do something official, there's a conspiracy, on and off campus, to ensure it doesn't succeed. The law of diminished responsibility." A sardonic smile enabled him to shrug it away. "There is in our society, inexplicably, you might like to say, a vested interest in failure. So I'm not going down that path. I'd like to hold council off, say everything's under control, not tell them anything, but actually appoint someone unofficially to look into it."

He raised his eyes. "Like yourself."

A Young Woman From China

Professor Ian Ferrier had seen it coming, but the blow still struck him in the midriff. He twisted in his chair.

"Why me?" he asked, in an exhausted voice.

"Because you're the right man for the job, Ian." The vice-chancellor liked saying things that were incontrovertible, like "because it's the right thing to do" and "the university expects no less". He had discovered that people were drawn into agreement with propositions that linked them (not precisely, when the links themselves became a matter of dispute, but indissolubly) with purposes beyond themselves, and therefore beyond argument.

"Ask not what your country can do for you, Ian," he brazenly intoned.

The vice-chancellor had been feeling about on his desk for a piece of paper, which he now scrutinised.

"China," he said. "The starting point is to assume that China is engaged, like everyone else, in the world's second oldest profession." He examined the professor's face diligently. "You would agree, that is what states do to each other?" He proceeded, as if confirmed. "Another assumption we can make is that China, with its large spread of overseas Chinese and students abroad, would rely on human intelligence rather than technology. It's called 'humint', I'm told, to distinguish it from 'sigint', or signals intelligence gained from technology. Australia relies on technology, of course, although we have our own version of 'humint', I understand." He was enjoying recently acquired knowledge, and then became serious, tapping the piece of paper in his hand. "The tawdry necessity of espionage should not blind us to the criminal activities alleged, for example, by a former Chinese diplomat, such as kidnapping and abduction of Chinese citizens in Australia. We need to keep a close eye on this kind of thing, Ian, and, if necessary, nip it in the bud."

He sat back and expanded his horizon.

"The issues, Ian, are bigger than class discipline and university inviolability. If people are being kidnapped and abducted, it is no longer enough for governments to solemnly declare that in the interests of national security they can neither confirm nor deny what illegal, inhuman and immoral acts their agents are performing in the state's name."

Professor Ian Ferrier knew he had no alternative. It was the last thing he wanted to do, sneaking and sniffing around for signs of rebellion or incipient terrorism, but he took the vice's point; transparency was not the way to deal with hidden dangers.

Something else was bothering him. He could not remember the vice-chancellor's first name or, rather, he knew that people called him Chip but he assumed that was not his actual name and he was not on such familiar terms with him to use it. In the old days, vice-chancellors were professional colleagues, but since universities had developed into huge enterprises they had become distant chief executives, grappling in fortress-like offices with inputs and outputs, forecasts and efficiency quotients, or travelling to Canberra to confront recalcitrant prime ministers and ministers of education and their underlings, or giving press conferences.

"Your professional knowledge will help," encouraged the vice-chancellor. "And being a single man will enable you to mix ... get around." His eyes scanned the ceiling. "In the evenings."

An unfortunate tendency was showing up in the student body, he remarked, dividing itself into local and international groups. The university rightly advanced the proposition that bringing students from Asia into Australia should help to improve Asia-literacy, but there was no sign this was happening. The foreign students hung out together, resenting the fact they had to pay full fees, living in shared accommodation in the same areas, which were even being called "ghettos". The locals resented the fact that classes were swamped with foreigners, many of whom had such poor English that their contribution to class discussion was barely understandable. Some of them (probably a minority, but articulate and from families often connected with Australian politics) were also peeved that the Australian story, whether history, politics, science, art or sport, was lost in the plethora of global issues.

"You can be a busy bee," said the vice, "collecting pollen from both camps."

"I was planning a trip to China in the next break," said Professor Ferrier.

If he expected this information to bring about a thoughtful pause or a change of conversation in his direction, such as, for example, an expression of regret, or even a suggestion that his new duties and the trip were not mutually exclusive and could be managed with a little administrative dexterity, he was quickly disappointed.

"You'll need to put it in storage for a while, Ian. I'd like to get this sorted out."

"But I've made the arrangements, and my itinerary has been virtually approved at faculty level," said Professor Ian Ferrier with a touch of testiness, tempered by the knowledge that what he said was not true.

The vice-chancellor smiled agreeably and waved his hands indiscriminately, as if he appreciated that he was placing a vast array of problems on the professor's desk.

"This is a university matter, Ian." The vice used the term "university" to elevate it above faculty, department, institute or any other form of campus activity. While he was quick to declare his appreciation of the work done at lower levels, he implied by his solemn tone that it was only at "university" level that the full range of human talent and responsibility was engaged.

He now resumed his mournful composure. He had had enough for one day. "Could we leave it at that? Nose about and let me know in a couple of weeks what you think needs to be done. There's a good chap."

The vice-chancellor accompanied his words with a rising motion in his chair, signalling that the interview was over.

Returning to his office, Ian turned over in his head the security issues that were now apparently his responsibility. He pondered on the behaviour of the vice-chancellor and his mysterious references to shadows and slips. What was all that about T.S. Eliot and pornography? He cursed his luck. Not only this lousy job, with its borderless responsibilities, but the trip to China put off.

He didn't share the vice-chancellor's gloomy view of the world. His own analysis was that global politics was in transition, from one dispensation of power to another, and change was often disorderly. He hadn't noticed signs of political tension in his class. There was a genuine flow of ideas and opinions. Perhaps someone was reporting to the Chinese authorities, but what did it matter? It was no skin off his nose. He doubted that anyone in Beijing would be interested in his mildly critical opinion of the Chinese political system. If they wanted to keep an eye on their own people, for their own perverted reasons, it was their business. It wouldn't make any difference to the way he taught or the way he assessed the performances of his students. The students knew that, so there was no overt politicking in class. They wanted to know, in their own self-interest, how the world worked and he was pleased to be able to tell them, as best he could.

You could quickly gauge the mood of a class, whether it was stable or fractious. Solitary, morose figures who sat in the back row and, if they did bother to take part, made sour, conclusive comments to which there was no rational response, were a worry. Each class had its ringleaders, style-setters. In his class, they were Renfei and Jian, who were like opposites, playing against each other, she thoughtful and accommodating, he sharp and purposeful. The balance of friendly disagreement gave the class a sense of security.

On the other hand, the vice had a point. If people were being kidnapped and abducted, or if there was serious tension between ethnic groups, something had to be done to stop it. But where was the evidence? What was the piece of paper the vice had on his desk that he seemed to be reading from?

8

At a Shanghai crossroads, as students from Tongji university straggled out for their lunchtime break, a small group of foreigners gathered in animated discussion. They were English teachers and their schedules had been suddenly altered.

"I won't do it!"

"It's beyond a joke!"

"They never gave the slightest warning!"

"They think you can prepare a new course overnight."

"It's because they're so disorganised."

"They're hopeless."

A slight young woman with large glasses twisted her body as she spoke. "Someone should speak to them."

A chorus of disapproval followed. Each appeared to be shouting at the others.

"They won't listen."

"They never listen."

"They do it on purpose."

The girl with the large glasses walked a couple of paces from the group and stood looking intently at a red-lettered banner, which was spread over the entrance gate. Several Chinese students began to gather at a distance from the angry group.

"I've been planning for months to go to Xian."

"They don't like us having the weekends off."

"I'd like to get my union organiser back home over here. She'd give them a fright."

The number of students increased until there were about twenty. They formed an untidy ring around the angry foreigners.

"I won't come here again. That's for sure."

"What happens if you just take off and leave them to stew in their own juice."

"They can stop you at the airport."

The girl with glasses and the restless body merged with the encircling students. A young man in jeans, black leather jacket and running shoes with thick soles stepped forward.

"Why don't you join with us, add your complaints to ours. Together we might get somewhere."

His English was very assured. It had rhythms that made the group observe him closely. The girl turned on her heel and looked at him.

"We have been told we must learn from the rigorous, competitive spirit of the West. So why not give them a model of a joint enterprise in action?"

The young man spoke quickly about the lack of heating in classrooms, about the failure of teachers to spend time with students because of their outside activities, especially selling their services to foreign companies, and of inflation, which made it difficult for students just to survive.

He laughed self-consciously as he finished, as if he sensed they had noticed he was well prepared. "What are your complaints?" he asked.

"The office told us today, Thursday, that we would have to prepare entirely new courses by Monday morning." The young woman with the glasses spoke as if she had completed an explanation, but her colleagues mumbled.

"That's just the tip of the iceberg."

"They're so inconsiderate."

"We've tried to reason with them but they won't listen. We've had enough."

"Tell me more," said the young Chinese leader. The phrase, with its intimations of irony and intimacy, drew them to him. The group and the circle merged. The girl with the glasses spun away from it, although still within listening distance.

A man of middle age, wispily bearded and plump, with a resonant American drawl, spoke first.

"What we're concerned about is Chinese education, per se." He went on: "The problem is that while the authorities say they want an open policy, in practice this is impossible. The examination system, by concentrating on testing memory and knowledge of authoritative texts, militates against free discussion. Also, the library, especially the audio-visual aids, and facilities, such as copying machines, are far below the standard competent teaching requires, indeed assumes."

He stopped, as if that might be enough. A woman with a European accent, coupled with an anguished expression and a rumpled dress, spoke as if in agreement with her American colleague.

"This university is famous for its German connections. Yet some students – most, I'm afraid – think Western education, indeed Western culture, is entirely American. Many of them seem to have gained their knowledge of the West from a mixture of Marxist textbooks and American television! So we detect a good deal of confusion in the minds of both education officials and students about what an open policy means."

She nodded in sympathy with voices of assent from her group.

"You realise there is a contradiction in what you are saying," the young man suggested. His measured manner was pleasing to the teachers and they listened. "On the one hand you are saying there is not enough open policy. On the other hand, you are saying, are you not, there is too much."

The girl tittered in appreciation. The group murmured in dissent. The young man went on. "Of course, contradiction is dynamic. But only if it is resolved."

The group stirred. Encounter with an old obstacle had revived in some an instinct for action, while others demurred.

"We are not ideological," the European woman said.

"It's not our business how the Chinese manage their affairs," a pretty English woman said. "Our interests are purely professional."

The American scholar emerged from judicious deliberation. "I doubt that it would be in our interests, or yours, to combine forces, as it were," he said, as if announcing a decision of the group, which it appeared to be.

"Perhaps you would like to know the result of our deputation, however," the young Chinese leader suggested. Some members of the group grumbled assent, in a display of courtesy.

"And we would like to know what happens on your side."

"Of course."

The two groups disbanded as the tension between them dissolved, shuffling away in sub-groups as if nothing had really happened, or as if they had been caught in some act they wished, without confidence, to present as entirely innocent.

The restless young woman approached the young Chinese leader. "I'm Andrea from Australia," she said, thrusting out a hand, which he dutifully took. "Liyong," he said. "Australians are welcome." They examined each other respectfully, like competitors in a game.

"I'd like to speak to you in private," said Andrea, walking away. He followed, motioning his intention to his group with one taut hand.

"I'm a Maoist," Andrea said.

"Oh, really." He responded as if he had never encountered an Australian Maoist before.

"The old kind," she said. "You want to use us to get at the authorities. I can see that."

"Yes, but why? That's really the point, isn't it?"

She lowered her face in a thoughtful manner, which was, she sometimes thought, attractive. "Are you a Maoist?"

He laughed loudly. "I knew you were going to ask that. I could see it coming." He looked at the ground and turned on his heel. "It's really sad."

"That's a new angle."

"I mean, having to ask. Of course, I'm a Maoist." He spoke lightly. "Mao was a great leader, the father of new China. He gave us victory over the Japanese, the Kuomintang clique, the Americans and the Russians. Every patriotic Chinese is a Maoist."

"Get serious," she said. "I mean a Maoist now, in relation to the ..." (putting up her hands and wriggling her fingers to provide quotation marks) "... 'present difficulties' or to quote some of my friends, 'dreadful state' we're in."

The young Chinese leader smiled broadly. "We live in interesting times," he said smoothly. "The capitalist tiger is bucking its riders."

"What you should know," she said, "is that they're all very unhappy people."

"I got that far."

"I mean personally. Their lives are a mess." She continued in her fierce way. "They're all escaping from something." She opened one hand, palm upwards and ticked off fingers as she spoke. "The American has no future in his university. The European is escaping from her husband. The tall one is having an affair with the wife of another foreign expert. The pretty blonde one fantasises about hairless Chinese young men and is terrified she will be caught with one of them and accused of being a spy. The little tubby one is gay."

She brandished her other hand as if the rest could also be ticked off, if he asked.

"What do you conclude from this?" The young Chinese leader had absorbed the information patiently.

"They're unreliable witnesses. They want more than they say."

"More what?"

"I mean less, actually. They're unhappy people and unhappy people like complaining. That's what I mean. No objective reality. No strategy."

"But this complaint about being told only a few days before is real."

"Oh, yes, but satisfying it won't make any difference. They'll find something else to complain about. They don't give a stuff about China."

"I happen to be interested in their particular complaints," Liyong said. He looked at her intently. "One thing at a time."

"Are you worried I might dob you in?" She was not looking at him as she spoke.

"As a Maoist you would probably understand why I would prefer not to answer that question," he replied seriously. "Even after you tell me what 'dob in' means."

She tried to explain shades of difference between nominating someone for an unpleasant task, contributing to a common cause and betrayal. His ironic features were undisturbed.

"I've got to go and mobilise the troops," he said. "Let's have coffee one day."

"Yes, let's," she said, "but don't rely on them. They're all bullshit."

"I'll watch my step." His quick step away matched his tone of voice. Then he stopped and turned. "By the way, I'm going to Australia."

She was interested. "When?"

"Quite soon."

"Why?"

He moved his head slowly back and forth, as if the possibilities were endless, then allowed their eyes to connect.

"I know someone."

"Where?"

"Melbourne." He gave a light laugh as he turned to leave, shouting over his shoulder. "We're going to ride in the trams."

On her way home she stopped as usual at a small market near the entrance to her compound, but instead of the usual cheerful bargaining with the peasant woman who usually served her (illegally, as she was not a licensed hawker), she found herself staring into space. The woman's fat brown hands darted over her stall, picking up things in anticipation, but the girl could not decide. The thought of the young Chinese leader filled her mind. Of course he was up to something. She grew excited, wondering what he was like as a person. He was slender in build, with a strong head and intelligent face. His mind was tough and supple.

She could never be part of his struggle. She was just a foreign observer, lucky to be on the fringe of things.

She wandered to the battered green pillar box where she posted letters telling of her adventures. How false they were, pretending that she was at the centre of great events. How silly she must seem, chattering about the importance of those she met and the significance of everything she did. She recoiled at the thought of reading the letters: she had asked that each be kept as a record of her odyssey.

When she reached the tree-lined walk to her own building, she hesitated for a moment, kicking the fallen leaves. Then she hurried, with her gaze determinedly at head level, to another cement structure, indistinguishable from hers except that it was not guarded by police. She climbed three flights and knocked on the door. A Chinese woman opened it, showing her surprise.

"Oh, it's you!"

The young woman was taken into a living room that served as a dining room, a bedroom and a study, indeed every imaginable activity except cooking and bathing, and placed in a chair with her elbows on a cluttered table.

"Please be seated," her hostess said needlessly. Two lidded cups of tea appeared as the Chinese woman placed herself opposite her guest.

She was in her late forties. A calm, weathered face suggested experience and the resolution of dangers and difficulties.

"I've made a decision," the Australian Maoist said.

"We've been through this before." The woman seemed disappointed. "You can't join the party."

"I know."

"Well?"

"I want to help China get back on track."

"How?" The Chinese woman's tone of voice was wearily mechanical.

"The world is awash with cynicism," the girl exclaimed. "And commercialism. China's being sucked in. It's got to take a stand on the true values of the revolution."

The woman lit a cigarette and inhaled smoke greedily. "China is full of people," she said, giving her mouth a humorous twist. "They're just people, like everyone else."

"How can you say that? Chinese civilisation is the oldest in the world. The revolution was a unique event. The collapse of communism elsewhere does not undermine the historic importance of what has happened here. The world outside is waiting for Chinese leadership." Her thin face was tense with expectation. "There's a perfect situation here at the university. It's Leninesque."

The woman drew on her cigarette impatiently.

"The foreign experts are at the point of revolt. The administration is creaking at the joints and the students are rebellious." Andrea mentioned her encounter with Liyong. "Bring the two together and you have a perfect ..."

"What?"

"Well, at least you've got a situation that, if properly managed, could tilt the balance ..."

"Tilt the balance! I've heard that before." The woman spoke drily, repeating the phrase for effect. "Tilt the balance. Very elegant. Did Liyong say that?"

Andrea struggled with the complexity of her companion's hostility. "Why do you treat me like a fool?"

The Chinese woman stretched across the table and patted her bowed head. "There, don't take it personally. Let's just say we're not in a revolutionary mood at the moment." She did not try to disguise her mocking tone. "You should go home and have something to eat," she said soothingly. "You're tired."

She stood suddenly and disappeared behind a curtain, returning breezily with a small saucepan, which she handed to the Australian Maoist. "Just heat it up." She bustled the young woman out without touching her. "It will do you good."

When the guards at her building stopped the young woman she was wary. She would deny having said anything. They were not advanced technically – microphones and tapes were of poor quality. It would be her word against Liyong's. Or the woman's?

"Australia on telephone," one of the guards said. "We not know where you are."

"Sure."

She nodded, waiting, her feet ready to twist, her body prepared for some emergency from the past, some experience she had excluded but not forgotten.

"They say no worries. They send telegram." Both guards smiled. "Your sister have baby," one of them said.

She stared at them, unable to smile in return. "Well!" It was an expression of acceptance and frustration. She turned and walked away, frowning and snapping her fingers, trying without success to bring a new world into focus.

9

THE PROFESSOR WAS AN AMUSED observer of his family rather than a member of it. He had kept in touch with his father for a while, but the whirling dervish had disappeared into a Mormon community in Utah, presumably in search of solace in polygamy or promiscuity. His mother's high-tension energy and social confidence were forbidding, so Ian settled for a life of his own, which unexpectedly developed into a study of international affairs. It began innocently enough; he was good at languages and interested in any other culture than his own. What seemed like a good life, for an intellectual dilettante posing as a university teacher, turned into a substantial career in a field crowded with threat experts, global strategic analysts and specialists in military hardware.

He had held his own, as his mother might have said, by keeping his wits about him. He noticed that a feature of the globalising world and its new technology was proliferation, whether of bombs, knowledge or political power, and while the quantity increased, the quality deteriorated. In research, findings were not adequately tested before being broadcast to the world; scholars tried to cover vast areas and were forced into higher levels of generality, or miniscule particularity. Intellectual opinions were as numerous, colourful and weightless as a backyard of balloons. Everyone was in such a hurry to announce the importance of what they were thinking, they had stopped thinking. Research had lost veracity; it was often disconnected bits and pieces plucked from the Web and cobbled together in a plausible format. He decided to concentrate on something that tantalised him because he did not understand it and he decided, further, not to engage in research but rather to sit down and think about it, explaining to himself in simple language what it was he did not understand.

So, while his colleagues were vying with each other to catch the latest global trend before it morphed into something else, jumping in front of television cameras with content-free hand waving, he published a little book that created a modest life for itself as a teaching tool. He thought of it as a slim volume of poetry on a shelf full of fat novels. Its title was *Modernity and the State* and in it he traced lightly the evolution of the modern state from the Westphalian treaties of 1648, which the experts had determined was its beginning, to the present day.

Great minds had grappled with the state, turning it into an enigma and transforming their exertions into political crusades. Some saw the state as oppressive and disposed to tyranny. Others regarded it as a progressive instrument that was intrinsically rational and would deliver humankind from prejudice and, through the welfare state, from poverty. He approached it without much more than curiosity, like a painter, a touch here, a touch there, searching for shapes and forms, shadings and contrast, but never straying far from the way it seemed in real life. The result was a clear-sighted description of something that had become as mysterious in political iconography as the Holy Ghost in Christian theology. And as powerful. No one seemed sure what the state was, but all agreed it was potent. It was "sovereign", a term descended from monarchs and the "divine right" they had inherited from God in a pre-secular era. Historic deeds had been undertaken in its name. Men and women all over the world died defending it. It monopolised the use of violence, deciding when force was legitimate and when it should be punished. It had a flag and an anthem, to which every citizen had to pay respect. Some anthems, such as the best known of all, the "Marseillaise", were bloodthirsty, although they were all sung by children with cheerful, innocent faces.

The professor's little book, unlike the Bible, the Torah and the Koran, presented no great truths but, like them in their lighter moments, it contained elementary observations, simply stated. The state, he pointed out, was not the nation. It was not the government. It was more powerful than either of them but it could not exist without both of them. The book's virtues were its simplicity, language that was tasteful and non-academic, and a bold ambition to trespass where only specialists had been before. It became a useful introduction to the arcane mysteries of statecraft. He was using it the night his battery went flat.

When he was writing his little book, the professor began to see Australia as a foreign country. You grow up looking out on the world from vantage points and barricades erected before you were born. A host of influences create your world: parents, peers, schoolteachers, what you read, see on film and television, hear in the lyrics and sounds of music. Now he tried to see Australia as others might see it, fitting it into the global jigsaw. What had before seemed normal – for example, that Australian soldiers should have been despatched to all corners of the earth to fight alongside the British, and then alongside their successors, the Americans – now seemed odd, as if they were mercenaries. Our soldiers in another country were a source of comfort for some, but were also a source of irritation, even hatred, for others. We thought our patriotism was moderate and good and that of our enemies was extreme and bad. When he turned to domestic Australia, his discoveries were no less disconcerting. What had before seemed sensible – for example, clustering our population in the south where the climate was comfortably temperate, leaving the bulk of the country as a kind of bolster between us and the rest of the world – now seemed eccentric. From most of the cities in Australia you had to fly for several hours across almost empty territory of your own before you reached foreign habitation.

He puzzled over the sacred role of war in Australia's history. It was widely believed that Australia had become a nation not when the British handed over political power in 1901, without a shot being fired, but in 1915, when Australian soldiers had been heroically slaughtered at Gallipoli, trapped in a strategic blunder by the British against the Turks. The camaraderie, sacrifice and bravery of war signified by the failed Gallipoli venture was celebrated in Australia with a kind of ardour he could not find in other countries, because they had other days of greater national significance, like independence, to celebrate.

He had been a quiet, fastidious boy, looking forward to a quiet, fastidious life. He had worked his way steadily upward at university, without engaging in office politics or becoming a public intellectual or a television celebrity or "doing something". Then, in mid career, his little book created an uproar. You would have thought he had accused his fellow Australians of not having "the ticker". A columnist claimed he was trying to turn Australian soldiers into pussycats. A representative of returned servicemen used the book as evidence that Australia was crumbling, white-anted from within. Some said his book was anti-American. Some said it was not anti-American enough. Some said it was evidence that Australia was falling under the influence of feminists, socialists, environmentalists and homosexuals. He was accused of appeasement, of pandering to one-world idealism and utopian pacifism and of preparing Australia to become a "people's republic".

Too surprised and bewildered to respond, he was relieved when a colleague wrote a review, reassuring the public that the book was merely a projection into the contemporary world of the "realist" view of international relations that had been responsibly held in all the major universities of the world at least since the end of the First World War. The reviewer cited Hans Morgenthau, Walter Lippmann, George Kennan and other worthy American pundits to show that the Australian author was merely another in a long line of credible thinkers about the ways of the world. He even cited Niccolo Machiavelli. According to the reviewer, it was because the "realist" view had been abandoned in Washington that the US and its allies were in so much trouble.

The professor was not so sure. Although he was not prepared to say so openly, being grateful for his colleague's defence, he believed "realism" was itself a problem, a snake pit of conflicting impulses. Held in check by prudence and good judgment, including respect for an adversary, it could be effective. Unleashed, and especially if coupled with religion, it took on extremist characteristics of the most "idealistic" kind, losing all sense of proportionality, including the sacrifice of lives.

Of the worthy realists the reviewer gathered in support, he was especially pleased with Machiavelli, who was a good writer. He went back to *The Prince* (George Bull's translation), savouring again the metaphor of the fox and the lion: "So (a prince) must learn from the fox and the lion; because the lion is defenceless against traps and a fox is defenceless against wolves." He knew the feeling.

A Young Woman From China

He walked one day near the Shrine, surrounded by memorials to war. There were plaques for every military action Australians had ever undertaken. There was an obelisk, representing "death and glory" with a Crusader's sword fixed on it, commemorating Australia's role in the Boer War 1899–1902, described as our first military expedition abroad in support of the British Empire. This was technically correct, as the Australian colonies had only combined to become a nation in 1901, but the professor knew that in 1885 New South Wales had sent a contingent of 500 infantry and two batteries of artillery to the Sudan to assist the British to avenge General Gordon, who had been murdered on the steps of the palace in Khartoum. They arrived too late to do anything: the Russians were creating trouble in Afghanistan and the British had decided to concentrate their attention there. The Australians asked to be sent to Afghanistan, or perhaps to India, or indeed anywhere the empire was threatened, but they were sent home seven weeks after they arrived. The episode stuck in the professor's memory as an example of Australian patriotism, heartfelt and inconsequential.

Then he came upon a statue representing a battle at Fromelles, a small village in northern France, when in one night, 19 July 1916, the Australian casualties were so heavy that they would later be recorded as the equivalent of those of the Boer, Korean and Vietnam wars combined. The statue, in gunmetal grey, represented a rescue mission after the battle: one soldier carried another over his shoulder. The inscription described how a voice had been heard in the carnage of dead and dying, crying out to the rescuers: "Don't forget me, cobber."

All the other statues and memorials retreated, sentinels of a history representing the failure of human intelligence, bringing destruction and tragedy on a grand scale, but the cobber memorial stayed in his memory.

He turned over and over Renfei's view of herself in China, not a person, just another one. In China, the psychologist's consulting couch and the small inner voice of conviction, whether religious or secular, belonged to another world. The individual was not important because there were so many of them. Was it possible that ignoring the anguish of self-realisation that the West demanded was more intuitive of the future, with global issues posing a challenge to traditional ideas of security? Cooperate or perish!

That evening he played his favourite collection of love songs – "Maria" from *West Side Story*, "Jeanie with the Light Brown Hair", "Smoke Gets in Your Eyes", "The Girl from Ipanema", "My Blue Heaven", "The Man I Love", "Every Time We Say Goodbye" and "Macushla". They brought tears to his eyes. He felt foolish and to cheer himself up played "Ukulele Lady".

Jian was not sure what to make of Knut, the Norwegian. He had only got to know him because he was often with Renfei, which did not make him any more acceptable. Jian was suspicious of European men who hung around Chinese students. They pretended to be interested in China, but they were really only interested in seducing girls far from home. It was a disagreeable fact of life that Chinese women were attractive to European men while Chinese men were not attractive to European women. He convinced himself that it had nothing to do with physical appearance. It was a hangover from the old days, when Europeans had power and wealth and could attract women, while Chinese were poor and the men had no appeal to women other than their own.

It was unfair, but the world was like that. Everyone bowed to power. If you had power, it was like having a million dollars in the bank, or like being famous or handsome. It might be different now that China was on the way up, but old habits persisted. Cosmetic surgery was a growth industry, making eyes wider, faces more narrow, lifting squat noses, straightening legs, building up breasts, all in the hope of looking European. People needed a bomb under them (metaphorically) before they would change.

Jian liked to put himself in Chairman Mao's shoes, launching a cultural revolution. He would have done it differently, taking care not to get the urban middle class offside. Mao was a towering figure, the leader of the greatest (in numbers) of revolutionary movements, but he was born a peasant and he never really understood the urban intelligentsia. Jian saw himself as a Zhou Enlai, born into local gentry, a diplomat, not a revolutionary, a genuine progressive, edging things along.

He was suspicious of Knut for another reason: he was too interested in Chinese affairs. "Nosey", the Aussies called it. He didn't get at Knut over every little bit of scandal in Europe, but Knut scrolled the Web all night looking for anything about China. He often came to class with news that they had not yet themselves picked up. He wasn't content with discussing the issues; he wanted to know what was behind everything, whether the vote in the central committee in Beijing had been five-four or four-five, the ins-and-outs in the party leadership in Shanghai, the nuances of Chinese culture and social life. All the secrets!

Jian was conscious of his family's history of service to the state, going back to the Qing dynasty in the 1870s. He felt responsible for China in a way that his friends didn't.

His great, great grandfather had been posted with a military contingent to Urumchi in Xinjiang province to put down a rebellion of Muslim Uighurs. His family had stayed there and his great, great grandmother had written stories about growing up in the "far west" that had been handed down in the family from generation to generation.

Jian was born and raised in Beijing and had never been to Urumchi, but Zhang family lore filtered down from its days in the west, a raw, warm memory, a reminder amid the splendours of Beijing that most Chinese lived close to the ground. Urumchi was built on an oasis and when the autumn snows fell it was criss-crossed with roads of mud. And there was the "honey pot" man, whose job was to scoop up the droppings of small children. In the alleys of the bazaars, small children were like animals, dropping their excrement in the mud. They wore bottomless rompers to make this easier and their backsides were pink with heat in summer and blue with cold in winter. Mothers were said to be envious and competitive about the droppings of their daughters. There was a tale that some girls were fed special foods so that their droppings were perfumed.

At school, his grandmother was given the "four treasures of the room of literature" – a brush, a brush stand, a block of ink and a stone ink slab. The brush was made of rabbit or sheep hair. She was taught to use the abacus. She saw merchants secretly bargaining by putting a hand up the other man's sleeve and by movements of the fingers indicating the price asked and accepted. She knew people who lived in caves made in hills of loess, the topsoil blown in from the desert. She saw wheelbarrows propelled by sails, camel caravans and yak carts. When a member of the family died, they were buried on their own land. She ran across crops of wheat, rice, sorghum, cotton, peanut, soya bean, rhubarb, liquorice, camphor, turnips, carrots, pumpkins, melons. A small seedless grape called turfan came from the Gobi desert. The famous Silk Road, starting in Alexandria and Istanbul, passed by Urumchi on its way to Sian and many people had mulberry trees and silkworms.

Jian's Urumchi stories left the impression with his friends that although his family was part of the Han transmigration intended to keep the Muslim Uighurs under control, they, like some Europeans sent out to run the colonies, had been seduced by the colourful local life and "gone native". But he staunchly supported Beijing's suppression of Uighur independence.

"The province of Xinjiang has been under China's control since 1755. Isn't that long enough?"

"But you said yourself that it's full of warlords and terrorists."

"It is China's biggest province and it has borders with eight foreign countries." Jian's raised hands suggested the complexity of the security situation. "Eight."

"Your favourite number," said Knut. Jian had a degree in mathematics and an obsession with Chinese lucky numbers. But he was thinking now of another kind of game. "Think of the opportunities for foreigners to play games inside China."

Their discussions always ended like this. Jian was convinced that China was peaceful "by nature", whereas the United States was "naturally" aggressive, interfering abroad in everybody's business under the guise of promoting liberty throughout the world.

"But democracy is good," said Knut, "and you haven't got it."

Jian agreed that, in theory, democracy was good, and China was working towards its own kind of democratic system, but democracy in the United States was a sham. He had been reading an article on the Web called "Inverted Totalitarianism" and it showed clearly how the United States, although seemingly a democracy, was actually controlled by money. You had to be a millionaire, or raise millions of dollars, before you could be politically active, because everything depended on advertising, especially television advertising. You had to compete with the latest in skin tonic or hairspray for the same audience, so you reduced your political message to a catchy phrase or jingle. Politics in America was just another form of marketing, not to be taken seriously. China might not be a liberal democracy, where people can say what they like, but at least it was concerned with serious issues, like economic development, housing, food and clothing.

"Democracy isn't everyone doing what they want. Democracy is majority rule. In China the vast majority of the people want economic development, better housing, food and clothing."

Jian then advanced his favourite theory. To do so, he needed to stand, whether because he was stiff from sitting on the grass or because he needed height from which to launch his thoughts was not clear, but the effect was to bring Knut also to his feet.

"Freedom has a high priority in societies with a belief in a spiritual life after physical death," Jian announced.

Some passers-by stopped, sensing a crank or, you never knew, someone with something useful to say, or maybe one of those performing artists who were all over Southbank on Sundays, doing amazing things like backward somersaults, tight rope walking or balancing a cap by its peak on the tip of the nose. Jian blushed, an unusual sight; his saturnine profile, which sometimes looked like that of an American Indian, flushed uneasily. He sat down, speaking in a low voice so that Knut was also forced to sit again.

"In India, freedom is rampant because everyone believes in reincarnation," Jian whispered. "They are all trying to score points for a better role next time around." He continued in a low voice, looking intently at Knut. "In Muslim theocracies, if you die a martyr you have virgins waiting for you in heaven. In liberal democracies like the United States you can die for liberty and believe that you will live forever, either in heaven or in the speeches of candidates in presidential election campaigns."

"And in China?" asked Knut loudly, concerned to dispel the impression that two foreigners were plotting on the grassy public space of democratic Australia.

Jian resumed his normal voice: "In societies with a grounding in materialism, like China, people know that there is nothing after death, so they concentrate on sustenance and survival in this life. That is why the basic human right in China is subsistence."

Knut contorted his features into a grimace that turned out to be a premonition of agreement. "Most normal, sensible people who haven't been infected with the religious bug know there's nothing after. But ..." he cut Jian short, finger aloft, "... we think liberty is part of normal, everyday life, not something you have a revolution for or go to war about." He stretched out on the grass and addressed the sky: "Something you live for, not die for."

He and Knut were sprawled on the grass opposite the Arts Centre, waiting for Renfei and Lu who were at an exhibition of French painting. It was a warm, sunny day and Jian was dressed neatly, as always, in long trousers and dark tunic, while Knut wore a football jumper, shorts with a crotch that swayed between his knees and boots that seemed not to have the benefit of socks.

They discussed football. They shared common ground in their attitude to Australia, a newcomer to the great international game that was called soccer in Australia. The fanatically followed local form of the game, "Australian rules", was falling behind in a globalising world, like American football with its "world series" that was played only in the United States. China, rising star in the new world economic order, was pressing its claim to football status against the game's firmament in Europe.

"The Australians are doing well," said Knut. "They are physically fit."

"But not agile," said Jian. "They are strong and fast, but stiff, not rubbery."

Their common support for Australia was helped by it not really posing a threat while offering at the same time an alternative newcomer to the United States, which was already too strong in sporting contests like the Olympic Games, as well as Nobel Laureates, defence budgets and per capita incomes.

"If it weren't for the African Americans in athletics and Jewish refugees from Hitler in maths and science, they would only be top of the tree in advertising and consumption of fast food," said Knut. "And maybe defence. And being able to listen to our conversations."

"But we're in Australia, a friendly country," said Jian. "Why would they want to spy on us?"

"It's easier on foreign soil," said Knut. "If it's in America, they have to get a warrant. But outside, they can do what they like." He looked about him, as if expecting to see evidence of all-powerful America.

"Why bother with a conversation about football between two students, not on anyone's list of the suspects who want to blow up the United States?" Jian was a cagey accumulator of information before taking a stand.

"If we were really planning something, we wouldn't talk about it openly." Knut spoke flatly, as if from experience. "We'd use a code language, like football. We'd have two teams, ours and theirs. And we'd talk about how to undermine their strategy and upset their game, while we were really planning how to blow them up. A soft target or a hard target, depending on what strategy we've adopted."

"They've got more important things to do," said Jian. He raised one hand. "I have an idea. China should join the cricket-playing nations of the world. It would be a strategic coup against the Americans, who want everyone to play baseball." He leaned over. "The Australian cricketers are waiting for China to join. They have a secret delivery called a Chinaman." He paused, a shadow on his face. "But China must act soon. The United States is using India to develop a new cricket game, which is just like baseball and good for television. When they are ready, the Americans will merge this quick cricket game and baseball and take over. China must only play the slow cricket game, which uses the secret Chinaman delivery."

Jian held up a finger. "The slow game is very strategic, played over five days. The turf and the weather are crucial. Each side bats twice, bowls twice. Very wide range of mathematical possibilities. Calculus of probability, good for Chinese numbers. Chinese people like games that are slow. There is a Chinese saying, 'waiting for the right moment.'"

Knut Harkken waited, caught between a lesson in Chinese numerology and a twinkle in Jian's eyes.

"The male is advised to push very slowly."

"Oh, yeah." Knut got the drift.

"Delay climax as long as possible." Jian moved into another gear. "In military and diplomatic strategy, Chinese tradition is lie low until the right moment, then suddenly stand up, frightening the opponent."

The two men shared the enjoyment of male supremacy in love and war, just as Renfei and Lu came running and laughing, hand in hand.

They had convinced themselves that the Impressionists and the Freudians had nothing in common. The Impressionists were harbingers of light; the

Freudians were fixated on darkness. They did not actually use those words. Lu said the Impressionists made you think of the sun, while the Freudians made you think of the moon. Renfei said the Impressionists were very "convalescent" while the Freudians liked living in a "brown study".

"I want to be a painter," said Renfei, tumbling on the grass. "Stop the world! Still life!" Knut joined her, playing her game. "I want to be a diplomat, save the world from war." Lu slid next to him, taking one of his hands and raising it above their heads. He did the same with one of Renfei's hands, while Lu proclaimed her ambition to the sky in a brassy voice, "I want to be a millionaire." Then she corrected herself. "Billionaire!" Jian eased himself gingerly into the vacancy between Renfei and Lu and followed suit, taking a hand from each and raising it above their heads. "I would like to discover the truth," he said quickly, as if not wanting anyone to hear. "Wow," said Lu and they all, except Jian, laughed. He chided himself. "Be a scholar."

They were spreadeagled on the grass near the flower clock, hands clasped, heads almost touching, feet pointing north, east, south and west. To a passing bird, one of the many spinning off after vainly circling the Arts Centre tower, they would have looked like an emblem that had been brought from the stark, rectangular building to nature's gallery outside.

The Zhang family had also inherited from Urumchi a connection with the Soviet Union, which in a roundabout way had brought Jian to Melbourne. A White Russian family escaping from the Bolsheviks had settled in their neighbourhood, among all the other immigrants from north, south, east and west – Tartars, Kasakhs, Uzbeks, Kirghiz, Mongols, Sibos and Tibetans, not to mention the Han people like the Zhangs who came in droves from China proper, promoted by the authorities in Beijing to keep the foreigners under control. The Popovs became friends of the Zhangs. When the Popovs eventually moved to Harbin and then migrated to Australia, the two families kept in touch and it was partly because of the connection that Jian decided to do his post-graduate studies in Australia.

The Popovs had prospered in Australia. Arriving at the time that able-bodied men were enlisted in the construction of the Snowy Mountains Scheme, they had worked their way through years of rising affluence, untroubled by the political and industrial tensions of the Cold War, and were now, in three generations, solid residents of Melbourne's outer suburban sprawl, commuting to each other from Croydon, Werribee and Knoxfield.

Jian had only the address of the grandfather of the clan, who was alive and well in Croydon. He trapped Jian for hours on his first visit in an argument about the merits of the Chinese case for the right to navigate the Amur river on the China-Soviet border, which had evidently been the big issue in Harbin when he was "in those parts". On his next visit he took Renfei with him, partly to impress her, partly to protect himself.

In the presence of a charming young lady, all was forgiven. Grandpa Popov had aged agreeably and was not disposed to chastise his young visitors for China's sins, past or present. He asked about the Zhang family, reminisced about their time together, made a few polite enquiries about Jian's scholarly progress in Australia, then settled down for a tour de horizon of what interested him. He viewed China's recent and dramatic ascent in the world, while poor old Russia struggled to put together the shattered bits and pieces of the old Czarist-Communist empire, as a historic reversal of power in the crowded northern hemisphere. A true perspective on mankind's future could only be gained from looking out (he was definite it was "out" and not "up") from the greatest country in the world for ordinary people, the working man and woman. Australia.

"A young couple like you should set up in Australia," he announced, oblivious to the confusion in their faces.

Australia had got it absolutely right, while the rest of the world argued and fought over bits of land and imagined interests and prospects. "Amour-propre," he said derisively, slurring his French in the Russian manner, as if affected by alcohol. Look at the Middle East, for God's sake! Land you wouldn't bother to bid for in Australia being contested as if it were a matter of life and death, because thousands of years ago some forebear may or may not have lived there. The Europeans had never had it so good, now that they had stopped acquiring territories all over the globe.

"The best thing that ever happened to Russia was when it lost its empire, all those stan this and stan that places," said Mr Popov, disposing of property with both hands. "Look at Japan! When it gave up trying to be like a European colonial power, it became the second most powerful economy in the world."

But none of them had been as successful as Australia, because none of them had given the working man his proper place at the top of the tree. In Australia, the "working man" (Jian noted that old man Popov had not caught up with the more recent Australian icon of "working family") was in command. The wealthy, corporate leaders, old-money families with inherited property, religious and regional communities and small business lobby groups all thought from time to time that they had the ear of government, but when it came to elections and budgets, the working man was king.

If you worked hard and didn't have ideas above yourself (which was half the trouble with the world) you could manage a perfectly satisfactory life in Australia. Mr Popov raised his hands to indicate the circumstances in which, in Croydon's salubrious clime, the perfectly satisfactory life was available to him and his loved ones.

The house was actually a weatherboard cottage, but had been recently painted and was substantial, having three bedrooms and what he liked to call his laboratory, which was an extension of the veranda, known by the previous inhabitants as a "sleep out". In retirement, he had taken up astronomy, the rational man's answer to religion. The interior of the house was cheerful, although Mrs Popov, before she passed on, had furnished it with velvets and plush drapes, as well as wooden ikons, that were out of sorts with its open sunniness. The grounds were extensive, but surprisingly occupied. The front was a vegetable patch, with carefully tended rows of carrots, lettuces and tomato plants, with clumps of rhubarb near a tank and clusters of melons and pumpkins everywhere, while the back was graced with birches and firs that everyone else in the street liked to show off in front of their houses.

"It's the sun," said Grandpa Popov, in explanation. The vegetables needed it, the trees didn't. The slope of the land was such that the front got more sun than the back. So he put vegies in the front and trees in the back. Being an Australian had taught him that the way to a happy life was to be practical.

"The rest is all show," he said, blowing it away. "Poof!"

The street was occupied by genuine Australians, most of whom had arrived before the Popovs. No one had followed his example, although the sun shone uniformly along the entire street.

"They will see the light," said Grandpa Popov, confident he had divined the essence of being Australian.

They listened respectfully to the old man, only leaving when it was getting dark. On the way home by train, Jian explained to Renfei the connection with his own family, and with the spirit of risk and adventure that still resonated with tales of Urumchi, before China became embroiled in the battles of the republics. Renfei listened courteously; she already knew Jian's story, which he often told in class.

They parted at Flinders Street station. Jian had a one-bedroom flat in the city. He suggested vaguely they could have a coffee in Federation Square. She declined with her usual excuses. She was uneasy alone with Jian. He lived an intensely motivated life, an "excellent person" but also a force to be accommodated in small doses, preferably in company with Lu and Knut.

10

THE PROFESSOR BROUGHT A SMALL desk into his office for Renfei's use. There was a spare desk in another room shared by two young women, but it pleased him for them to be together. He wanted to be near her, to hear her voice, perhaps to feel the warmth of her hand, even to touch her. He was scared of the consequences if he allowed this feeling to take over, but he could not resist it. Renfei had that effect on him. The strange thing was that although he hardly knew her, he trusted her, which he had never felt strong enough to do before.

"I've got something to tell you," he said, raising his voice to give himself courage.

It was winter and she had arrived that morning wearing the hat that Mrs Winterbourne thought made her look thrilling.

"I'm afraid my China trip is off. The university has given me some work that will tie me up in Melbourne."

"But I have told my parents."

"Well, not off for good," said the professor. "Later in the year. Postponed, you might say."

Renfei pouted. "I was captivated by the idea of you visiting Lijiang, with the possibility you would encounter my parents." She subsided, looking glum. "What about my job?" This was a side of her he had not seen before, protecting her interests.

"I'll find some work for you to do here in Melbourne." Indeed. And now was the time to tell her what it was. She was wearing a pale blue, tight-fitting sweater with a low neck. He could see the top of her breasts, which were plump and white like her knees. "By the way," he asked, in his casual voice, "do you think it likely that your government has agents planted in our class, reporting back on what Chinese students say?" He laughed over his self-consciousness. "Or what I say?"

She did not hear him, or chose to let it seem that she had not.

"Did you hear what I said?"

"Yes." She was smiling to herself.

"Well, what do you think?"

"Of course."

"You mean people are reporting what is said?"

"Why not." It was not really a question.

"You seem sure," said the professor.

Renfei explained. She was sure in general, not in particular. The government in China wanted to know what everyone was thinking and one way of finding out was to get people to tell them. Students needed money. So ... She raised her hands in explanation of everything and anything.

"Who in our class would want to do it?" He tried to sound as if the question were presumptuous and an answer unnecessary. "By the way, I like to dance." He was about to exert his authority, or the vice-chancellor's, and he didn't want her to think that he was just a part of the power structure.

"Anyone, not just Chinese, maybe an Australian. Maybe Knut."

"He doesn't need the money. His government is paying his fees. And a living allowance, I'm told."

Renfei shrugged her shoulders. "Do you really like to dance, professor?"

"The vice-chancellor had me in the other day. He's concerned about inter-library loans." That should bring them back on the rails.

"Inter-library loans?"

"Making bombs. That kind of thing."

"You get that stuff on the Web," said Renfei.

"Yes, I know. The vice wants me to check, make sure no one in our class has done anything ... silly. I thought you might be able to help me."

That was enough. Leave the thought with her. He would pick it up in a couple of days. For now, he needed to deal with her disappointment that he would not be seeing her parents in Lijiang.

A Young Woman From China

Professor Ian Ferrier called across the room to Ms Liu Renfei. "The simplest way of solving the immigration problems with your parents is to marry an Australian citizen."

Renfei busied herself at her desk, ignoring him, making a show of printing something from her computer. The task completed, she sat back and looked at him.

"Are you making a wedlock proposal, professor?" she said cheerfully.

At that moment, the professor was actually thinking about refurbishing his unit. His building was one of those that fell unnoticed between what was old and solidly built and new, stylish and minimalist. It's virtue was, as the auctioneer had proclaimed ad nauseam, "position, position, position", being close to St Kilda Road, the Shrine, the Royal Botanic Gardens and Fawkner Park, yet tucked away from traffic streams and clanking trams. It had two bedrooms and a third room that could be a bedroom or a separate dining room but which he had made into a study, lined with books (as was the guest bedroom, rarely used). It suited him perfectly, but he wondered whether he had become so comfortable that it was like the Volvo, and his slippers. They tugged at his heartstrings, while their utility declined.

Perhaps not a major restoration, just a splash of paint to brighten things up? A new piece of art? The paintings on the walls were from the "tonal" school, all blending in with each other, with an effect that was dull, although he had chosen carefully and the quality was good (and the value added over time was reassuring). The carpet, a conscientious grey, and the tweedy curtains were there when he bought the unit and he hadn't paid attention to them since. A few changes here and there might spark the place up. It needed to express his personality, not the previous owner's. But as soon as he said it, he knew he would not be able to make the necessary choices of colour and texture, because he had no idea what his personality was. He did not think of himself as having a personality. Entertainers had personalities, which they thrust at you ad nauseam. He was an educator, dealing with matters more important than personality. To do his job, he needed to be impersonal. He thought of himself as a human being trying to understand, trying to find the answer to the oldest question of all, the right way to live. Personality had nothing to do with it.

"Did you hear what I said, professor?" Renfei tapped at the keyboard, not raising her head.

"I'm sorry," said Professor Ian Ferrier. "I was thinking of something else."

He was thinking about the little book's reception. You would have thought by now that its ideas would have been picked up by a new breed of politicians keen to make an impression. For example, the idea that Australians needed to be Asia-literate. "You could make it work politically only on one condition," said John Burnside. "We become Asia-literate not because we wish to understand their cultures, and certainly not because we intend to adopt them, but so that we can keep them under control. Learn their languages, study their religions, get inside their heads, but so that we can advance our interests against theirs, not become more like them. The way the British trained Arabists to manage the Middle East. And not at primary school. At that stage all you need is a simple patriotic narrative. Maybe at secondary level, but not too much. Only when their minds are fully formed do you give them intense language and culture studies." Johnno's smile was poised between cynicism and sadness. "To provide recruits for Australia's intelligence agencies!" It was hard to tell with Johnno whether he was joking, but what he said rhymed with public sentiment. The only development that would force Australians to become Asia-literate was if Asia became so prosperous that Australians had to learn their languages and understand their religions and cultures in order to make a living.

He wondered about Australia. Old habits of deferred pleasure and endurance, forged in the bracing air of the antipodes, had been abandoned in favour of the latest international fashion. The old kith-and-kin instincts had almost gone. Mateship had become no more than a caricature of blokey politics. Australians had willingly fallen to the temptation of affluence, which was to seek pleasure in hothouses isolated from nature and available only to the wealthy. From the United States, we imported an obsession with money and fame. From Asia, we imported cheap clothes and machines, but nothing in the way of ideas or institutions that might add value and quality to Australian life. This would not matter if we had our own core values of fortitude and stamina, our own model of social cohesion and civic pride that could withstand the torrent of making money and selling things, but we didn't. Ex-politicians, sports stars and entertainers vied with each other to promote products on television. Without shame, a former captain of the Australian Test cricket team, a position once only slightly below high public office in the eyes of traditionalists, spruiked for a brand of beer.

The clamour over climate change was typical. Even his mother was saving energy, turning off lights in the house, driving at low speeds and not braking abruptly, worrying whether it was environmentally responsible to be cremated. He wouldn't go as far as Charlie Boy, but he shared his scepticism. The scare wouldn't last. Australians were addicted to speed and comfort and any political leader who tried to wean them away was doomed at the ballot box.

Perhaps he should forget about Australia, become an expatriate, living in exile, which allowed you to be an Aussie without having to live with any of the consequences. Bali was a possibility. When he was preparing for his first visit he read a travel brochure that described Bali as "a nasty fleshpot of cheating, dope, prostitution and crime", but when he got there, he saw only fresh faces, gentle, swaying bodies and direct and dignified eyes. They had worked out how to enjoy life's pleasures without artificial stimulation. The nasty fleshpot was a creation of Westerners, mainly Australians, who swamped Bali with their version of pleasure.

If he lived in Bali he would write essays about what he saw and did. He would explain why, when he first saw a brick wall in a green field, he told himself that if he did not get out of Bali on the next aircraft he would stay there forever. It was his first visit. He knew no one, had barely noticed the stylised thin carvings, the Buddha-like statues, the entanglement of human forms, flora and fauna that the Balinese believed was nature and should be made into art. The emotional effect of the red brick wall and the greenery filled him with longing, the same kind of longing he had felt when he first read Eliot's "sunlight on a broken column". He could not explain it, but he felt it.

"I asked if you were proposing marriage," said Ms Liu Renfei, glancing in his direction.

As she repeated her question, an idea unfurled itself before him, with the strength and elegance of a double helix. It was natural, not foolish, one strand affirmed, to seek a companion in life's journey. The other strand asserted that Renfei was not just any young woman, from China or anywhere else, but a person of quality and integrity, worthy of his trust. Entwined, each strand supported the other. He tried to force them apart, so that each could be tested on its merits, but they clung to each other, refusing to be separated.

His aversion to having to share living space with another person was trivial, the double helix declared, rearing like a charmed serpent. Why was he bothered by the thought of sleeping with someone in the same room, not to mention the same bed? And the bathroom? Surely it was not beyond the wit of an intelligent man to manage dual access to a bathroom? Being irritated at having to clear the crumbs left on the kitchen bench by someone else plumbed the depths of shallowness, if that were not itself a contradiction. Of course, he needed a workroom, as a companion might also, but was it beyond the realms of physical and financial ingenuity to find somewhere to live with work room for two people? Or space for two cars?

The defence that a benefit of living alone was being able to work in pyjamas on mornings he did not have to go to the university was absurd, the double helix protested. Was it not humanly possible to find a companion who did not object to him working in his pyjamas or, indeed, might want to do the same? People managed to live together. You might even say it was normal; most people preferred the comfort and convenience of company to the freedom and independence of solitude. Was it not a fact that he often felt the need for conversation and had he not worried lately that he might become arid from too much introspection?

Man was a social animal. And marriage and children were no longer the dead-end they used to be. People moved and the family adapted. His mother and Charlie Boy were proof of that. The Burnsides and the Morewitzes had arrived at their comfortable situations from several directions and, who knows, might disperse again. Indeed, marriage and children were a form of security, forging connections with the outside world that acted as a kind of support system for everyone. A single person, by contrast, had to take the initiative to make social connections. You could make a case that being single was more onerous than being in a family, where responsibility, like power in the contemporary world, was shared.

A Young Woman From China

Come on, spat the double helix, be honest! All that reading of Freud on Leonardo da Vinci about the role of dominant females in the lives of left-handed homosexuals was a pose. You are neither left-handed nor a genius. You are attracted to women. You can be stopped in your tracks by the sight of a woman's face, especially if she has red lips; you allow your imagination to relish what it would be like to lose yourself in her. True, you are socially timid. In conversation, you often back away, finishing up fending her off in a corner. But aren't you tired of these stealthy visits to so-called massage parlours (in the afternoon, when no one is watching, after which you live in fear that your mother will find out). Monogamy is not natural. Life is full of tasks, small and large, that conveniently can be shared and challenges, major and minor, for which two heads are better than one. And you like children and they are drawn to you. In trams, you catch the eye of a bundle in a trailer or on a mother's lap or a father's back and you provide a laborious wink, to the infant's delight and the proffer of a pink finger. Even with Gillian's brood at family parties, you are the one who dances with them, swings them up to the rafters, makes funny faces they try to mimic. Children appeal to you, not just because they are soft and cuddly, but because they are lively and eager, full of importance at the beginning of life's journey.

So what's holding you back? Don't tell us that it's because your mother keeps prodding, as if you would be out of the starting blocks as soon as she stopped. Ah, yes, trust. You have convinced yourself that women cannot be trusted. Even when you are drawn to a woman because of looks or intelligence or some obvious talent, you believe they are, in some way, incorrigible. They will follow their own instincts, even when they have committed themselves to an objective, position or plan. They will find a way of satisfying something else of themselves, while protesting they do not realise it is contrary to what they have declared they will do, or say, or not do or not say. They are the "weaker" sex, indeed, and by pleading ignorance or weak-mindedness or simple forgetfulness, they artfully get away with whatever they want. They want security and comfort, and they will change their allegiance (from one man to another, if that is the source of their security and comfort) to make sure they get it. They will not take a stand, or a leadership role, on the great issues of the day because they want to keep their options open (in case the other side wins).

The voice of the serpent became softer, as the second strand, more subtle and resilient than the first, took over. Did you say they cannot be trusted? But you trust Ms Liu Renfei, don't you? From the moment you met, you have trusted her, and you haven't been disappointed. You have often remarked that there is something about her that moves you. What is it? She can be attractive, of course, but you are not interested in anything as superficial as good looks.

Perhaps you are averse only to Australian women, especially Australian women who move in the same circles as Mrs Winterbourne. Asian women are said to be more faithful, less ambitious, content to be cook and bottle-washer in a traditional family arrangement, while having also a head for business. You don't see yourself as paterfamilias? You don't want a traditional family arrangement. You want a partner who is your equal, who can discuss ideas and issues, who is as involved as you are in making fine judgments about life and work, who is, in other words, as committed as you are to finding the right way to live. You are seeking a companion on the journey of life. Of course you are. That's what all the great minds, whether in art or science, come up against eventually, after they play games with the latest invention in science or the latest innovation in art. The right way to live!

Have you not noticed that Ms Liu Renfei has embarked on a journey of her own? Because she is young and in a strange land, she may seem at times to be unsophisticated, but you have yourself remarked on her maturity. On human rights, for example, is she not grappling, in her own way, with the same issues as you? She understands, like you, that just because human rights are universal does not mean they are abstract. It means rather that whatever they are thought at any time to be, they are available to each and every individual. While it is true that an individual's rights become "human" through relations with others, it is difficult to know how they can be implemented except as individual rights. She knows, as you do, that it is individuals who make decisions about their lives and bear responsibility for those decisions. It is the individual who secretly marks a ballot paper and places it in a box. It is the individual who is conscripted or enlisted, is honoured or discharged from service to the state, who takes the oath in court, who is required to go to school, who graduates, is employed or receives unemployment benefits, who is taxed, fingerprinted or DNA-registered and a photograph of whose face is on passports, driving licences and other forms of identification. And it is the individual who is tortured, held hostage, executed, set free.

She knows all this, just as you do, although she comes from an entirely different culture. And she is beginning to wonder whether it is the conscience of individuals that is the mainspring, indeed according to some the source, of morality. You can see all this happening in front of your eyes, as it were, her struggle to understand, and you are moved by it, moved by her.

So what's holding you back?

Professor Ian Ferrier stood, braced his shoulders, remembered Fromelles, glanced at the open doorway of his office, stepped smartly across the space to the desk of Ms Liu Renfei and lowered himself on one knee with bowed head before her.

"I was only joking," she said.

The professor's body slumped or, it could be said, relaxed, preliminary to a rearrangement of limbs that enabled him to stand erect.

"All I am proposing is lunch," said Professor Ian Ferrier.

11

WHEN ANDREA, THE AUSTRALIAN MAOIST from Tongji University, Shanghai, returned to Melbourne she went straight to her old friend, Gillian Jones (nee Winterbourne). They had lunch in café bar 181. Gillian had renovated a terrace house nearby, installing a lift ("for my old age") and was well known at the café, where she liked to lunch before going to the studio for her evening show.

They had been friends at school, which was just a short walk from where they were now. The café was long and narrow, opening into a small, private enclosure at the back where Gillian liked to sit. Having greeted each other at the street entrance like the long-lost friends they were – "Hi Andy" and "Yo, Gilly baby" – they offered a contrast as they made their way to the back. Gillian was smart casual in business grey, with short, straight blonde hair and a confident manner. Andrea was bundled in gothic red and black and peered suspiciously at her surroundings from behind big spectacles.

As soon as they had given their orders, Andrea made her intentions plain. "I want to go on television and tell Australians a few home truths about that deceiving, thieving gang in Beijing."

Gillian was used to Andrea's opinions. She had come to school with a scholarship from the western suburbs and was convinced multicultural Australia was on the brink of becoming a republic. She wanted not only a popularly elected president but also a rewriting of Australia's constitution, inserting a Bill of Rights and including a reference to the nation's sovereignty as indelibly resident in the Australian people. As nothing happened, Australia's political parties being unenthusiastic about gearing up for another failure at changing the constitution, she had taken up China as the hope of humankind. While Gillian was sharpening her wits as a presenter in the television business and reading Jane Austen at home as a gesture to feminism, Andrea decided that if the Chinese were to take over the world they would need to speak and write English properly, and took off for Shanghai.

"I thought you were a fan."

"I was, but they've turned into plutocrats, no better than the Americans. Worse. At least the poor deluded Yanks believe in what they're doing. The Chinese are just using capitalism as a form of crowd control, keeping the masses in line."

Gillian was more accomplished and certainly more successful than her friend, but she was not at ease with politics. She winced at Andrea's language.

"Everyone is so busy making money they have no time for anything else, including thinking for themselves," said Andrea. "So the boys in Beijing are sitting pretty. The system is self-regulating."

Gillian thought her friend needed an elementary lesson in television values. "Our viewers are not into ideology."

"You can say that again." Andrea had done some research, viewing a couple of Gillian's programs in preparation for their lunch. "They're into this," she said, displaying a newspaper she was carrying. The front page was almost completely occupied by a picture of a missing boy. He had been last seen "hanging out" in the Fitzroy Gardens. There was speculation that the gardens had been "taken over" by gangs who preyed on boys. In broad daylight! The tone of the article reflected a sense of outrage that all self-respecting readers were expected to share.

"Takes people's minds off the big issues," said Andrea. "Like the boys in Beijing." She was determined: thinking was important in politics, even if Gillian couldn't see beyond show and tell television and bodice-ripping, chick lit romance.

Gillian suggested that the media did not control events, merely responded to them in a way the public could understand. "The human angle, that's what interests people. A missing boy is news. And the story might reveal something about the society we live in."

"And tug at the heart strings," said Andrea. "And give prejudice a touch up." She was so sour they both laughed.

"News we can use." Gillian was trying to be helpful. "We can bring in an expert, or a neighbour, to give background. We get a lot of news from public relations people who can see something in it for their clients."

"There's plenty of angles on China," said Andrea. "China's in the news every day."

"Yes, but blasting away at the Chinese government isn't our kind of television."

"You mean, don't bite the hand that feeds you. The big end of town is in bed with the boys in Beijing."

Gillian was battling the impression, fostered by the print media, which was in financial trouble because classified advertising had dried up, that television was just a medium for corporate advertising. She restated a well-rehearsed position.

"We're not into propaganda, for or against. We don't bother with the Falun Gong people, or even the Tibetans. Everyone knows their situation. The pros and cons have been gone over time and time again. It's not news."

"Well, is it news that China's teachers are fed up with their terms and conditions and having to toe the political line?"

Gillian was doubtful. "Rebellious teachers are not news. We have them here all the time. And toeing the political line? We have that here too." Honest brokers like herself tried to stay out of politics. "The trouble is, you stay out of politics and you get dragged into history. The black armband view. All bad. Or the plucky cobber view. All good. History isn't great television." She offered a mild correction. "Unless it's about the past of a famous person. Or war history. Digging up old battlefields." She considered. "Auctioning war medals?"

Andrea was not prepared to give up. "The teachers are fed up because what they're teaching has no connection with what's happening outside the classroom. The kids know it, the parents know it. Even the so-called communists know it, but they can't admit it because they haven't got a doctrine to explain it. It's like the Catholics and birth control. Once you accept birth control, the doctrine that every child is God's gift collapses."

Gillian sidestepped birth control. "We're not into right-to-life. One program on that and you're never finished. This view, that view, it never stops."

"That wasn't my point."

"I know, but why is it I feel the need to remind you?" Gillian's smile was intended to glide over the surface of a relationship that went back a long way.

"You think I'm a dill, don't you?"

"No, just out of touch."

"With the world of glitz and glamour? I plead guilty."

"With the real world." Gillian touched the hand of her friend, who was beginning to look angry. "The world of feeling!"

Andrea looked her most disapproving. "The world of feeling is a world of sentimental pap."

"You look down your nose at us workers in the television industry," said Gillian with a laugh. "You're up there with your great thoughts about the fate of the world. Like the preachers and the politicians, committed to dogmas and doctrines, policies and programs. Telling us how we should live. We're down here, embedded in ordinary people. Telling the world not how to live but what it feels like to be alive."

"What it feels like to have your boobs lifted," said Andrea, with a smirk.

"Yes, and what it feels like to go to jail or be thrown out of your house by your bank or lose your most loved one or be unable to have children or suddenly have a lot of money or be terrified of being raped or frightened of dying or not able to sleep or stop snoring ..."

Gillian raised her hands in the air to convey the endless prospect of human feelings.

"You think it's a game, a money-making game. It's not fun, I can tell you. You're dealing with real feelings, not emotion or sentiment as writers and painters and musicians think it is after they have worked it into the shades and shapes and forms that art and the art-loving public demands, but the real thing, off the street, raw and brutal." She shrugged. "Or just plain silly."

Andrea was surprised by Gillian's intellectual conviction. "I'm disappointed in you, Gill. I thought you were just in it for the money."

"Look," said Gillian, serious. "The money's great. But the thrill I get out of it is showing people like you who you're dealing with – real people. We give them a voice. Provided it's not a political voice, or ideological, or requires heaps of research and documentation to establish that it's accurate. Nothing clinical or analytical. No serious investigative journalism. Just a voice."

"Like a cat that's hungry or a dog that's been hit by a car."

"A human voice, thank you. And we do investigate. But not spending weeks wading through documents or checking what some politician said a year ago. Foot-in-the-door, that's our style."

"Nothing that might suggest that what distinguishes humankind in the animal kingdom is the size and scope of the brain." Andrea was doing her best to be scathing. "Just the senses. Just feeling."

"You can be as contemptuous as you want, but it works. It's what the ratings are all about, what the advertisers pay for. People want to see themselves on the telly, not some big-head know-all, not some politician feeding them a line. Ordinary people like them."

Andea was spared further insight into television's humanitarian mission by the arrival of lunch. The two women discussed mutual friends and Gillian's latest venture, which was to open a gym.

"Everyone's into working out." She appeared to be responding to a criticism. "Why not? Keeping trim makes sense. It's healthy, and you look good." As Andrea, who was not only trim but looked as if she would benefit from a good meal, did not respond, she continued: "People have to look after themselves." Andrea still failed to show interest, so she wound up: "Well, it's better than the bloody Pacific."

"How is Charlie Boy?"

"No improvement."

Gillian had once told Andrea that her father was on the verge of dementia. She wasn't sure whether it was degenerative, like Alzheimer's, or just a reaction to "that pestering woman" but the deterioration was perceptible. She had spoken to the best medical people in town about it, but she had no power to do anything. "Mrs Winterbourne" (puckering her nose in distaste) made sure she wasn't able to get near him. The most she could do was telephone with a few useful suggestions. But he never answered the telephone and she had to explain everything to "her".

"He's besotted with some Chinese girl she brought into the house. He gave her Vonnie's car."

Andrea tried to show sympathy by nodding her head. Veronica's suicide was a well-known part of Gillian's story, like the fashion model's flight to Berlin.

"He would love to see the grandchildren, but I have to get him out of the house to arrange it." She mused for a moment on ways of slipping her father past Mrs Winterbourne and then turned to her favourite subject.

"Tara is so grown up, you wouldn't recognise her. A little miss." Gillian left a "little miss" undefined, but it was obvious that she was proud of it. "Damien is a real boy, into everything. And Lola is simply a darling. She melts your heart."

"My sister's just had a baby," said Andrea.

"Good," said Gillian, trying to remember the sister's name. Her children were a source of wonder to her women friends. They could not understand how she managed to be so crudely fertile and remain a television celebrity.

"It's not natural to have small families," she told them. "The rich and the poor have large families. The poor can't help it and the rich have the means to manage it properly. It's only the middle class that tries to keep the number of children down, because they live above their means, sending the children to expensive schools, indulging in luxury hobbies and international holidays, living in mansions they can't afford."

"You're not anti-choice, are you?" her friends asked, a feminist chorus.

"Of course not. But it's not natural not to have children, or to have only one child."

She repeated all this, more or less, to Andrea, whose response was that the one-child policy in China contributed to savings, one of the reasons why the country was economically successful. But Gillian had the bit between her teeth, as Mrs Winterbourne might have said. She was her father's daughter, riding full tilt at every shape and shadow of orthodoxy.

"I'm with George Bernard Shaw. The undeserving poor and the undeserving rich provide the genetic pool of innovation, the engine of progress. The deserving poor and the middle class want security and stability. One-child families will reduce China to suburban villas and shopping malls."

Andrea brought the conversation back to Gillian's television program.

"Is it news that the Chinese government is planting spies in the classrooms of Australian universities?"

"It certainly is."

"Well, they are."

"But how do we make it news?"

"Get off your backside and find out." Andrea was unsparing. "It's called investigative journalism."

"I've explained. We don't have the time for that."

"Well, I'll say it." Andrea had moved on. "That's news, isn't it?"

"If you're a good source. How do you know for sure that's what the Chinese are doing?"

"Everyone knows they're doing it." She slanted a grin at her friend. "Except Australian television." She ticked off on her fingers several more or less reputable public statements by people who were in a position to know.

"The boys in Beijing have been studying history," said Andrea. "They know that most of the anti-colonial leaders got their ideas and the confidence to implement them when they went to Europe to study. At home, discipline was so tight it never occurred to them that rebellion was possible." She smiled bleakly. "The boys have got the people at home under control with bread and circuses, but they're worried that young Chinese studying abroad will pick up wrong ideas and return, as future leaders, to cause trouble."

Watching Gillian's face, Andrea knew she needed to provide her story with flesh and bones. Even a name. What was Liyong doing in Melbourne? He had told friends he was working at the consulate. He was up to something. He wouldn't be Liyong if he were just issuing visas and stamping passports. If he had a real job in the Chinese consulate, why didn't he say so in Shanghai?

"They've sent down a student leader, Wang Liyong, to do the job in Australia. I got to know him well in Shanghai."

Gillian's eyes ceased looking for somewhere to escape and rested on Andrea's face.

"How well?"

"We were lovers."

Intellectually, it was true. Their minds were on the same wavelength. And she had often wondered what he was like personally. She had imagined them as lovers, revolutionaries against the world.

"Really." Gillian was interested.

"Struck the right note for you?"

"I'll have to check with my producer," said Gillian, looking suddenly professional. She surveyed her friend, clear-eyed and calculating.

"If you think we're trash, why grace us with your presence? Why not write a clever op-ed piece for the newspapers. Then you can use your favourite language and the ideas that are too complex for the likes of us?"

"I want to appeal to the masses," said Andrea, twisting her lips.

"You mightn't come out smelling like roses," said Gillian.

Andrea shrugged. "You're an old friend. You can look after me."

Gillian engaged in a series of contorted physical acts, which involved closing one eye, turning her head on one side, standing and creating a frame with her hands through which she made snap judgments of Andrea. She appeared not to be entirely satisfied.

"Are there others we could interview? Members of a group perhaps?"

"Just me, I'm afraid."

"I wouldn't want our viewers thinking it was political."

"Well, it is."

"Yes, but if the story is human, the politics won't be noticed."

"You mean you want a tear-jerker. Aussie girl looking for utopia meets Chinese spy who breaks her heart."

"Something like that," said Gillian.

12

"My boyfriend in China is here," said Ms Liu Renfei. The professor looked up from his laptop, unsure if he had heard correctly.

"Here?"

"In Melbourne." Renfei gave one of her "So funny!" smiles.

The professor was determined that his surprise should not overwhelm his relief, which was substantial. He had begun to think that the boy, having got into trouble and, if he was anything like Renfei, refusing to confess (perhaps not knowing, anyway, precisely what he had done wrong), had finished up in some prison. Or having had a fright had drifted into calmer waters, never to be sighted or heard of by his little group of political activists again.

But they were together, apparently, in Melbourne. "You must be pleased." Despite his best effort, there was a question in his voice.

"Of course." It was almost a reprimand. Could he have thought otherwise?

"What happened, after the arrest, or whatever it was?"

"They made a mistake." Renfei was anxious to clear up any wrong impression the professor may have gained from their previous conversation. "You remember I told you they said that if he had done anything wrong he would know what it was. Well, they kept asking him and he kept telling them he had done nothing wrong, so he couldn't tell them what it was." She gave her "that's the way it was" look, with shrugged shoulders and hands in the air. "So they gave up."

"What's he doing in Australia?" His tone was polite. It would be indelicate to inquire why he had taken so long to get in touch with Renfei, and then unexpectedly turn up in faraway Melbourne.

"He's a diplomat!" She agreed it was a surprise. "Wonders have not ceased."

The boyfriend, whose name had still not been uttered, had been posted to Melbourne in the consular service. "If you were making your visit to China," Renfei said, "he could arrange for you to get a visa quickly. You would not need to stand in the sun and rain with everyone else." There had been articles in the newspapers about the popularity of China at the time of the Olympic Games, when long queues at the consulate had attracted the media.

He decided that humour was in order. "I hope I will have an opportunity to meet him, without having to queue up at the consulate."

"I will arrange it." Renfei was all courtesy and efficiency.

When Liyong had telephoned her, she couldn't speak. "It's Liyong," he said in English. "I am in Melbourne."

She remembered the rhythm of his English, so polished, everyone said, without the broad vowels of American English, you thought he must have lived in England. She remembered his eyes glinting, his lips full and thrusting, his rambling eyebrows.

"Liyong," she said, in wonderment. "I could not lose the smile from my face," she told the professor.

"I am most anxious to see you." Liyong sounded confident, as if there was no need to explain his lengthy and mysterious absence. "You slipped away." As if it was her fault.

"How did you get my number?" she asked.

"I'm working at the consulate." He continued to speak in English, but his laugh was the same as it was at Tongji, ironic and intimate. "The consulate knows everything."

She could see him in his jeans and black leather jacket, balancing on his runners. He was like a movie actor, always active, talking, moving. "Well!" she said. "Fancy you being in Melbourne!" Suddenly, everything changed, Lu and the flat they shared, her classmates, the Winterbournes, the little red car, the professor, herself, Melbourne and its trams, the Pacific Ocean. Everything. Her past had caught up with her.

"Fancy Liyong being in Melbourne," she said to the professor.

Everything was coming together around her! And it was all because she had come to Melbourne, and was living here, meeting real people who were not Chinese, trying to understand what was happening in the world, working out her future in it. Now Liyong was part of her journey.

"If my parents were here, it would be so amazing I would just lie down and die," she told the professor.

She calmed down after the first shock. It was just the surprise of Liyong suddenly appearing that made everything seem different. He was her first and only boyfriend, and she had been faithful to him in Australia, although there was no commitment (and he had disappeared without a word). She had been faithful to the idea of him, someone from her hometown whose instincts she understood without needing to have them explained. They came from the same place. They knew what a soft wind was, a strong sun, a green valley with hills in the background, trees lining long straight roads. Even political instincts. He did not have to explain to her what he was doing as a student activist. She knew how he felt, the boy from Lijiang in the teeming metropolis of Shanghai. You had to stand firm, thinking your own thoughts, or be crushed in the rush.

"Have you been back to Lijiang?" Renfei asked Liyong.

"Not recently," he said. "How are your parents?"

"They are very well, thank you. And yours?"

"They are in fine spirits."

"Fancy Liyong being in Melbourne," she said again to the professor, her eyes wide with excitement.

Liyong arranged to meet her at the Grand Hyatt coffee shop. He said he was staying somewhere cheap nearby until the consulate could find him a suitable apartment. He paused when he said "suitable apartment", and she imagined he was thinking of something big enough for the two of them. He was already in the coffee shop when she arrived. He stood up, one hand extended. She brushed it aside and kissed his cheek. She had never seen him in a suit and tie before. He looked older, taller, bigger. She was wearing the hat that Mrs Winterbourne said made her look thrilling, and swinging a shoulder bag. He had never seen her in a hat before. She looked smart and eager, as if she wanted to be part of the world around them in the coffee shop.

Each knew they owed an explanation to the other, but Renfei's was easier. She had tried to find out what had happened; she had kept making enquiries even after she arrived in Australia. It was only after she had given up any hope of making contact with him that she had stopped. Liyong, on the other hand, seemed to have vanished from the face of the earth.

She said all this to Liyong, then asked, "How did you get a government job and be posted to Melbourne?" She was hoping he would say that he had asked to come to Melbourne because she was there.

Liyong toyed with his tea. "It's a long story." He was lost in the past, his eyes hazy with detail. "They made a mistake. When they realised this, they talked to me about my student activity, my beliefs. I told them honestly. I had nothing to hide."

"So you weren't really arrested and taken off to prison?"

"Not really."

"Why didn't they tell me when I asked about you?"

"The people you asked probably knew nothing about it." Liyong smiled the way she remembered. "The bureaucracy is not as efficient as you think. One hand doesn't know what the other is doing, but neither likes to admit it." He lounged a little, trying to settle in the small, rigid chair. "You're supposed to know, without being told." He shrugged and lounged deeper. "And even when you're told." He left the impression that there was much you did not know, even when you were told.

His face had hardened a little, she thought; his jaw muscles were tighter. She remembered his cheek had been soft to touch, even when he hadn't shaved.

"So they just instinctively recognised your great qualities," said Renfei, adopting the flippant style they had used when they were together in China.

"Exactly."

"So why Melbourne?"

"Can't you guess?" He fixed her with eyes that teased, then invited.

"I would like you to tell me," said Renfei, demure as a spring daisy.

"You are here."

"I was hoping you would say that." Renfei lowered her eyes, then quickly lifted them, with the devil behind them. "What other reason could there be?" She dropped her eyes again. "It has been so long."

"I thought you must be having a good time in Australia. Time passes quickly when you're having fun."

She wondered what he meant by "having fun". It was not a phrase she had heard in Lijiang, nor even at university in Shanghai. He must have picked it up in Beijing. She was sure he would have met many girls. He looked so satisfied, lounging in the chair. Was that what he meant by "having fun"? She responded bluntly.

"If what you really want to know is whether I have another boyfriend, I haven't, Chinese, Australian or anything else."

He chuckled. "Have you been studying in a convent?" She tried to hit him across the table with her bag.

The rest of the afternoon passed like a dream; she could believe at times that she was back in Lijiang. They met again in the early evening, after he had completed his appointments, had a Chinese meal in Little Bourke Street, then went to his hotel. She waited in the car park while he collected messages at the desk, and took the lift directly to his floor, where he was waiting. "Have to be careful," he said.

In his room, they ignored preliminary endearments and enticements, simply placing their bodies at the disposal of each other as if that were the purpose of being together. Renfei was reminded of the pleasure of being Chinese. She delighted in his smooth skin, the contrast of black hair and pale, ivory face. Her mother had said that Han Chinese smelled different because they did not eat cheese. Although her mother had been making a distinction with Tibetans and Uighurs, Renfei now convinced herself that she had for two years been living among a people with a distinctive smell from which she was now offered blessed relief. As they held each other again and again, in spasms of embrace, she asked her ancestors to forgive her for any harsh judgments she had made of her country and its people. Finding her way in a new country, she had sometimes forgotten what a privilege it was to be Chinese. Her mind filled with images of kites flying in a blue sky over Lijiang, where she could live with Liyong in blissful ignorance of the rest of the world forever.

When Liyong asked her if she could find the time to help him with his work, her heart jumped a beat. "Of course." He was asking her to share his life. She made plans in her head. She would stay in Australia as long as possible, so that they could return to China together when he had completed his posting. They would be married in China properly, after their parents had had a chance to meet. It would be a big wedding. It would bring more happiness to her parents than a visit to Australia.

The next day, they met in the afternoon at his suggestion at the Republic café, opposite the South Yarra railway station. He explained on the telephone the best tram or train connections for her. She was surprised how quickly he had got to know Melbourne.

He had changed. His manner was official and purposeful. He wanted to know if she had many friends, whether they were just Chinese, or other foreigners, whether she had met any interesting Australians. "I understand that you have some kind of employment with your professor?" She told him, wondering how he had learned. "Paid?" She told him, wishing she hadn't. "How much?" She gave him the details, including deduction for tax. She told him of the limit of twenty hours work a week for international students. He questioned her about her classes, the number of Chinese students, how critical they were of China. Were the Chinese students under pressure to respond to a pre-determined, liberal intellectual agenda, antagonistic to Chinese values? He said he wanted her to report to him on her classmates' attitudes to issues that he would provide her with, and update regularly.

Then he looked at his watch and announced that he had another appointment.

"Go for it," said Lu. "What have you got to lose?" Liyong had said not to tell anyone, but she had to tell Lu or she would burst.

Renfei listened to her friend in silence. She was not surprised. Lu would try anything. Renfei, on the other hand, was "flabberboozled" that Liyong, who had contempt for the authorities when he was a student leader, was now working for them in this underhand way.

"It's just a game," said Lu. "It won't make any difference to the big picture. If you can get yourself a few brownie points, why not?"

"What are brownie points?" Before Lu could answer, Renfei said that Jian could get into trouble if she told Liyong what he said sometimes. "Why don't you warn him off," said Lu.

"I can't. Liyong said I wasn't to tell anyone. I shouldn't have told you."

"Why did you?"

"I had to tell someone."

Lu nodded. "Yeah, I know. Or you would burst." She laughed. "I will burst if I don't tell my boyfriend."

They were silent, contemplating the mystery of the human need to communicate.

"Don't say a word," said Renfei. "Or else." She placed an edged hand at her throat, symbolising the end of Lu's earthly existence, but the gesture only caused a fit of the giggles, from which they emerged clinging to each other.

"This job with the professor," said Renfei. "I'm not sure what he wants me to do. He keeps hinting that it isn't just the translating, but he won't say what it is."

"You mean the professor wants you to tell him what we talk about outside class?" Lu was quick as a tack when you didn't say what was in your mind.

"I don't know," said Renfei. "It just popped out. Must be a Freudian slip." She and Lu collapsed into giggles again. But Renfei was still bothered. "Is Liyong a diplomat or a spy?"

Lu was delighted that their discussion in class had connected with the real world. Perhaps the professor was not so airy-fairy after all.

"Your boyfriend wants you to tell him what we say in class and your professor wants you to tell him what we say outside class. You're really in trouble!"

13

Renfei took Liyong to Argo Reserve, hoping it would remind him of Lijiang. She had discovered the reserve walking one day from Chapel Street on a leafy path called Lover's Walk that ran along a railway line through streets of neat cottages and small blocks of flats. Something about the area appealed to her and she wanted to share it with him.

The cottages had front gardens, usually lemon or olive trees, grape vines or climbing geraniums. The people who lived there had decided as a community to keep it the way it was, protecting themselves from development. The reserve itself had a past. People passing through liked to stop and talk, like they did in Lijiang, and there was also a commemorative plaque provided by the local council. It had once been the site of a large house and grounds, run by a Quaker family as a refuge and training centre for "women in need" (meaning just out of jail) and later for "wayward girls" (meaning wards of the state). All that remained was a red brick laundry, which on her visits was always locked, where the girls had worked, and high red brick walls that still blocked off much of the site. Whenever she came, she would sit listening to the birdcalls, imagining they were the voices of the wayward girls.

A garden of gerberas had been established in a simple arrangement of brick flowerbeds, laid out around a pond to catch the full range of the sun and at a height convenient for propping up elderly or disabled residents out for a stroll and in need of a rest. There was a children's playground, with slides coloured blue and yellow, and a supply of plastic bag "dog scoops".

At the centre was a spreading Moreton Bay fig tree and on a grassy mound an Australian gum tree, from which birds chirped a welcome. On her first visit, she sat on one of the benches to soak up the atmosphere, feeling happy and secure. She liked the word "Reserve" and tried it on her tongue several times. It sounded dignified. She could see the sky all around her. It made her feel safe. Urban squares that tried to create a sense of space while surrounded by tall buildings that blocked out the sky made her nervous.

Liyong was puzzled by the location, although he sat patiently while Renfei extolled its virtues. "It's very relaxing, don't you think?" She sat with her hands folded and beamed her pleasure around Argo Reserve to make the point. A magpie warbled agreement.

"Like Australia," Renfei said.

"Australia?" When Liyong felt superior he liked to take a cigarette from the packet he always carried and light it, which he did now.

"Australians don't expect everything to work perfectly."

Renfei struggled with an idea that had barely formed when she expressed it. "Getting it half right is alright." She was pleased with her formulation but Liyong raised an eyebrow. He thought everything in Australia seemed to work efficiently, although, compared with China, infrastructure and equipment were old.

"Oh, yes, everything works well, but they don't mind if it doesn't." She resumed her appreciation of the surroundings. "Like Lijiang," she said hopefully.

However, Liyong had another view of Australians, which was that they were obsessed with what they called "world best practice", which was really "Western best practice" and took no account of progress made in China.

"The Olympics gave them a shake. It showed that China was not only a superior sporting nation but also a modern power."

"It was sad," said Renfei, "when that little girl with the good voice was taken out of the opening ceremony because she didn't look right and they gave her voice to someone who looked right. They got the perfect result. But it was sad." She did not want to seem critical. "Didn't you think?"

"Sad?"

"For the little girl. And maybe for the other girl, too, because she will always know it wasn't really her."

Liyong said that the opening ceremony was a multimedia event, an artificial construct, so finding fault because a bit of it wasn't authentic missed the point. It was designed to have a certain effect, which it did, most successfully. The whole world was impressed. No good Chinese girl could argue with that, and Renfei remained silent.

Liyong leaned over to touch her hand, both a reassurance and a reminder of the intimacy in which he had earlier asked her to help him. "I'd like to get results soon on that matter we discussed." She acknowledged his touch with a light smile, continuing her benign surveillance of the little reserve.

"There's something to be said, don't you think, for not asking for too much," she said. "I sometimes felt in China that I was being asked to be too good to be true."

"The government has to set the bar high, to encourage the people to jump as high as they can, but they don't expect everyone to succeed." Liyong had become expert in public policy and the need for government to take account of the weak, foolish and wicked among its citizens, as well as the virtuous, obedient and responsible.

Renfei wandered off to fondle bright orange gerberas. "Shouldn't you put the bar low, if you want to encourage people to jump?" Liyong seemed prepared to consider the possibility, but Renfei was wandering farther away. "Don't you feel sometimes that it would be great not to have to strive, just to live a simple life, enjoying simple pleasures?"

Liyong stubbed out his cigarette on the brickwork. It was stand and deliver time. She remembered the student leader at Tongji.

"China has embarked on the greatest journey in our history. This is our moment of destiny. For centuries we have been powerless to stop others doing whatever they liked with us. Now we can shape our own future. To say that what you would really like is a nice quiet life is an insult to ..." If he had said "me" Renfei would not have been surprised, but he said "our country". She had been reprimanded and was quiet.

Liyong gestured. "Bringing me to this quaint spot to tell me that Australians are not up to the mark, but you think they've discovered the secret of life – not to strive but to enjoy simple pleasures – surprises me." He softened. "Are you trying to tell me something?"

"Not really." Renfei had actually brought him to Argo Reserve because she wanted to share with him a place she had discovered for herself. It was not in the tourist brochures, none of her friends knew about it. It was a real piece of Melbourne and it reminded her of Lijiang. Well, it wasn't having the effect she expected.

"That matter we discussed," said Liyong.

"There is something I need to tell you." She crossed her hands and settled into her "that's the way it is" look. "I have been thinking."

"Is that unusual?" Liyong was charming when he teased.

"I can't do what you asked – about students in class."

Liyong was perplexed. "I thought we had agreed."

"Yes."

"I have informed the consulate."

"I said I would think about it."

"Yes, but what could you possibly have thought about other than ...?" Liyong spoke as if she had not agreed immediately only because it was obvious that she would agree eventually.

"I have been thinking about it."

"But we agreed that you would stay in Australia until my posting was over, then we would return together to China to get married, after our parents had met, and ..."

"Yes."

"But ..." Liyong had slipped into the reassuring logic of "could only mean". Their plans to marry when they were back in China could only mean that they would continue their relationship in Australia, which could only mean that she would do what he asked to assist him with his work.

"My friends could get into trouble," Renfei explained.

"Not if they are true Chinese."

She examined him with a hint of detachment. "They do not want to overthrow the government. They are not plotting to blow up something or assassinate someone. They are just discussing these issues in class because the professor has set tasks for us."

Liyong had heard this sort of thing before. "The ideas that emerge from these class discussions are not favourable to China. They are not favourable because the questions are framed as a conversation between liberal democrats. China is not a liberal democracy. It is communist, a developing society using capitalism to pull itself out of poverty by its own hands."

"So?"

"It is the duty of true Chinese to defend China against these charges from people whose experience is different from ours. How can a professor whose outlook has been formed from viewing the world from Australia understand what is at stake in China?"

"He would like to visit China," said Renfei.

"He is welcome, if his intention is to improve his knowledge. But let him not tell us how to run China. Tell me this. Has he introduced you to the concept of the greater good?" Renfei slowly shook her head, trying to remember. "Of course not. He has filled your head with the freedom of the individual. But as you know, every Chinese understands that in China the rights of individuals are subject to the greater good of the community."

Renfei decided to lower the temperature. "I did not think you were interested in his opinion. I thought you were interested in the opinion of the students."

"We are interested in the effect on young Chinese people of studying abroad. We do not want to stop it, but we are concerned at the effect it is having. We do not want our leaders of the future, who have the huge task of developing China so that it is strong and can withstand foreign pressure, to be distracted from their duty by ideas they become attached to while studying abroad." Liyong fixed Renfei with a penetrating look. "Foreigners do not want us to be strong. They want us to be weak so that they can do what they like with us. They know that if we try to be a liberal democracy overnight, the way they want, we will be weak. If Tibet is independent, if the Uighurs are independent, if every unhappy or dissatisfied person in the country has the freedom to dissent, the strong China that is emerging now will collapse. Then the foreigners and their companies can move in and take their pick."

It was the theme of her schooling. It was the hidden agenda behind every official statement. It was in every Chinese mind. Disunity is death. If we wish to prosper and be safe we must be united. Renfei reached for a compromise.

"But if a student's name is on your list of people who are suspected of not being patriotic, their future, and the future of their families, is threatened. They can deny it, but they will not be believed. You are police, judge and jury, everything."

"We can reason with them," Liyong was not in a mood to compromise. "We can persuade them to change their minds."

"If you put them in a cell and do all those things to them."

"Do all what things?"

"No sleep, electric shocks. Torture."

"That's just lies in the Western media."

Renfei composed herself. "I am feeling anger in your direction, Liyong."

"Because I speak the truth?"

"The truth you speak is not kind to human beings."

It was Liyong's turn to wander away. He had learned that if you wished to succeed in politics you needed to keep up the pressure. If you hesitated or indicated that you would consider a negotiated settlement or anything less than you were demanding, you would lose. How to keep up the pressure on Renfei?

"Anyway," he said. "The Americans use torture. They have written books about it. They call it the shock doctrine. With electric shocks they wipe everything from the mind, then they put into the mind whatever it is they want. That is how they get confessions."

"At least they admit later they were wrong."

His negotiating logic had a weak link. Renfei seemed to be holding in reserve the option of remaining his lover without doing what he wanted to help him with his work. Liyong decided to rely on her need of him. He could well believe that she had had no lovers in Australia: she had come to him like a thirsty animal to water. "Where have you been?" she had cried out. He had smiled to himself. A good question.

"If I am not successful in my work, I will be sent back to China."

Renfei had come prepared for such an eventuality. "I am in readiness to return to China."

Liyong had not seen this side of Renfei before. She was not the pliant young woman he remembered. He resorted to jealousy. "Perhaps there is someone else in your class who would like to help. Your friend Lu, for example?"

"Don't you dare ask her!"

"Why not? She's old enough to answer for herself, isn't she?" Liyong's stern expression did not permit him to leer.

"She will do anything, just for fun. Or money."

"She may wish to show she is a true patriot."

Renfei felt cornered. She looked around for somewhere to retreat, but the door of the laundry was, as always, padlocked. The wayward girls of Argo Reserve and the wayward girls of China combined in a chorus of helpless discontent.

Liyong moved towards her, but she rose quickly and brushed him away.

"You should go," she said. He looked around amiably for an exit sign. "Where?" She pointed in the direction they had come.

"You can get a tram to your office."

"Renfei!"

"No, go!" She stood rigid, pointing. Whenever he tried to speak or move toward her, she raised her finger and pointed imperiously.

"It's no fun being in jail in China," Liyong said.

Renfei waited, not trusting herself to speak. Was he threatening her, or telling her something? She could tell from the way he faced her, irresolute, that he was hiding something.

"So you were in jail?"

"I thought you knew." He spoke as if the difference between what was known and not known was unimportant.

"You said you were not."

"I don't think I would have said that," said Liyong. He was checking the record. "No, I'm sure I would never have said that." He appealed to her. "I've been through a bit." He scuffled his feet and twisted away to light another cigarette.

"You lied," said Renfei fiercely.

His response was lost in a billow of smoke.

"They put you in jail, broke your head open and let you out to do dirty work."

Liyong listened with his back half turned away, as if to shield himself from her words. He was preoccupied with extracting a sprig of tobacco from his cigarette. His confidence had subsided, while hers had risen.

"You're not a diplomat," said Renfei calmly. "You're a spy."

"I'd better get back to work," he said.

"Yes," said Renfei. She nodded in the direction they had come, her imperious finger limp at her side.

When he was out of hearing, she called after him. "I'm over you." It was a phrase Lu liked to use. Then she sat among the gerberas and cried.

14

"How is Liyong?" the professor asked.

"He is not the same." Familiar with Renfei's modes of expression, Ian waited. "He is not the person I left to be himself in China." Her voice was flat, her eyes downcast.

He nodded wisely. *Tempus fugit, tempus omnia revelat.*

The professor speculated. The vice-chancellor's faith in him as a single man roaming student haunts at night was misplaced, but he kept his eyes open. Often the evidence stared him in the face – arms around each other's waists one week, sitting rows apart the next, not daring to look at each other. It was their time of life, when nothing was permanent.

"I'm sorry."

She looked at him with obsidian eyes. "For what are you sorry? Or who?"

While he was working on his answer, she told him. "You should be sorry for Liyong."

Ian had no idea what had happened to the idyll of Lijiang, but he felt obliged with students, even with Renfei who was almost a real person, to keep a perspective. "Bureaucrats may seem fussy and overbearing, but it has been wisely said that bureaucracy is our protection against the misuse of power."

Renfei raised her eyebrows in disbelief. Lu was right about the professor.

Ms Liu Renfei and Professor Ian Ferrier were meeting at her suggestion in café bar 181. It was near his unit and she had become familiar with the timetable of the No 8 tram that stopped at the corner. There was something she needed to discuss with him "in secrecy" she said when she rang to make the appointment.

It was sunny, with a light breeze blowing from the bay, but the professor was muffled and coated in preparation for a howling gale. "You can never be sure about the weather these days," he said, glancing at the sky as they took their seats. Renfei smiled, a seasoned Melburnian. She was wearing black stockings and sequined shoes and a woollen jumper that allowed her arms to be bare. They sat outside. She preferred being with people, part of the community as in China, not out of sight tucked away in a corner. She liked to watch people doing exercises in parkland across the road, just as they did on the old Bund in Shanghai.

"Some lazy bodies are still having breakfast," she whispered, looking around.

Four girls, mysteriously absent from a nearby school, occupied the table next to them, alternating shrieks of laughter and alarm, and making occasional sorties across the street to a prefabricated metal toilet painted green. They wore grey woollen stockings and flat brown sandals and when they were in one of their bouts of hilarity, heads together and arms around each other's shoulders, they could have been mistaken for a confederacy of some kind of large bird.

"There is something I have to tell you," Renfei said. "I am unable to do what is in your mind."

She had considered her options carefully. If she were not prepared to do Liyong's dirty work, it followed that she could not work for the professor. He had not yet actually asked her to do dirty work, but she could tell from his behaviour that it was in his mind. She wanted him to know how she had come to her decision. All might be fair in love and war, as they said in English literature, but not in the relationship she had with the professor. If they were not truthful with each other, her time in Australia would have been wasted.

So she told him what had happened at Argo Reserve. She avoided the emotional bits, including the lonely ending, but left no doubt in her account that she had turned Liyong down. She summarised as accurately as she could his arguments for assisting the Beijing authorities and her arguments against, allowing the professor to make up his own mind about motives. She ended with Liyong on the prowl, looking for someone else to do his dirty work.

The professor was fascinated. The realist theory of international relations was being played out under his nose. He could see the vice's face. The temple of academic freedom was under assault.

"Do you think he will ask Lu to help?"

"He will leave no stone turned down."

"And will she help him?"

Renfei shrugged. "Lu will do anything."

"Will she tell you if she tells him?"

"She tells me everything. But now she might be ashamed. Or she might tell everyone in the class!"

The professor considered his position. She seemed to be balancing what Liyong wanted against what the vice-chancellor had in mind, but had not the former demonstrated the need for the latter?

"You can't put what Liyong wanted and what I might ask you to do in the same basket," he said.

"You haven't actually asked me yet." There was a suggestion of a pout. "I'm just guessing."

The professor apologised. "The truth is, I had this meeting with the vice-chancellor and somehow things just fell into place. I was hoping that they would fall into place again." The professor looked sheepishly at his hands. "I was hoping the whole thing would go away."

He presented the vice-chancellor's case lightly, glad to be rid of it. There was a wealth of difference between spying for a government, when your information could mean jail, even execution, for those you named, and "passing on" in confidence anything "untoward" that she might pick up in the "normal course of events". He wasn't interested in political opinions and he was confident the vice-chancellor wasn't either. But if anyone was planning to bring guns into class and take hostages, or anything along those lines, surely she would be doing everyone a disservice if she knew and did nothing about it.

"What if you discovered that someone was going to come into class one day and blow us all up?" he asked, with his little-boy look.

"Is he a suicide bomber, or does he leave the bomb in the class while he pretends to go to the toilet?"

The professor had not got that far.

"If he is a suicide bomber, I would not be close to his thoughts," said practical Ms Liu.

"Excluding the suicide bomber for the moment," said the professor suavely, "would you inform the authorities?"

"I would try to persuade him not to do it."

"And if he declined to be persuaded?"

"I would tell him that I had to inform the authorities."

"Which would mean he wouldn't do it?"

"Yes!" Renfei was delighted with the professor's logic.

"Or he might just postpone the day – and not tell you next time?"

She struggled with the implications. "Perhaps he would give up."

The professor drained his café latte at a gulp, as he always did, after examining it morosely, twirling the glass in his fingers, waiting for it to cool. "Shall we take a walk in the gardens?" he suggested.

He had decided on this earlier, as part of a strategy to put what his cruder colleagues called the "hard word" on Renfei. The exigency was uncalled for, but he still liked the idea. She might put her arm through his. She didn't, but as they strolled past the Nymphaea Lily Lake she stopped suddenly and confronted him with one of her searching looks.

"Do you know about the greater good?"

He waved with both arms to the four corners of the earth. "We are in the midst of it!"

She was delighted. "I thought you would know about it."

"The Royal Botanic Gardens is the perfect example," he announced. "Public space cared for as if it were privately owned."

Miss Liu received a short history of the gardens. Successive generations of civic leaders had preserved them as a tranquil public space against commercial pressure from an expanding city, while at the same time developing them as an educational and scientific enterprise. If asked to justify the "elitist" nature of the gardens, which did not attract huge crowds

144

in the way that beaches and sporting arenas did and were cheek-by-jowl with another elitist establishment, Government House (a relic of the days when Australia was a conglomerate of colonies run by governors despatched from the ruling social and military circles of England), authorities relied on the "lungs" argument. A city needed the breathing space gardens provided. But the "greater good" argument, if anyone had thought to present it, was much stronger, the professor thought. The quality of life in Melbourne was lifted a notch higher by having the gardens in their midst, as it was lifted by having a river or an art gallery or an orchestra or a streetscape admired by everyone.

Renfei was examining the back of a bench, painted red like several others, on which was a brass inscription. "Who was Dorothy Campbell?" she asked.

The professor shook his head. "Her love of the gardens was second only to her love of Melbourne," Renfei read aloud. She moved to another bench: "When I want to regain my sanity, I come to the gardens." And another, dedicated to someone "Who knew the value of a good place to sit." She laughed. "So funny." And, further: "To the world you were one. To us you were the world." And: "One rose was picked, With that rose, An eternal paradise was created."

She stood thoughtfully, looking into the middle distance, took a few paces toward the bank of the little lake, did her pirouette, then ran to another bench. "We sought refuge from a troubled world. And found it here." Excited now, she ran to another, the professor trundling in her wake. The brass plaque on the bench was larger than usual to take a longer than usual inscription, which had faded in the weather. She turned to him for assistance. He read, panting: "Give me my Romeo: and when he shall die, Take him and cut him out in little stars, And he will make the face of heaven so fine, That all the world will be in love with night, And pay no worship to the garish sun."

"OMG!" Renfei exclaimed. She had learned it from Lu, but did not know what it meant.

"Shakespeare," said the professor. But she was off, running to several benches facing the Ornamental Lake. "Morning has broken, like the first morning." The next seat was dedicated to a young couple who had died together a few months after marriage. She tried to imagine the circumstances and why their friends had thought to donate a garden bench. Then: "For Jane, who loved these gardens /And for Peter, who always sat beside her."

"OMG!" She was frantically signalling to Ian, who strolled over and read it out for her. "The kiss of the sun for pardon/ The song of the birds for mirth/ One is nearer God's heart in a garden/ Than anywhere else on earth."

She took the professor's arm. He had been waiting for that. They strolled like a couple, she grappling with the surprising knowledge that the sane and sensible people of Melbourne put these astonishing thoughts on public benches.

"Do you know what OMG stands for?" She shook her head.

"Oh My God!" He gave it an exclamatory lift. "You should be careful, or people might think you are religious."

She squeezed his arm. She was grappling with another surprising thought. She had rejected Liyong and ended their relationship, while she and the professor seemed to be closer although she had also rejected him.

"I am sorry that I cannot be of assistance to you," she now said. "But it would spoil our relationship, which is precious to both of us." Her face was flushed with expectation, although Ian remained silent. "What is in the dark depths of your mind?" she asked to encourage him.

"If I were to tell you what is in the dark depths of my mind you would not believe it."

"You could try." Renfei was surprised at her boldness. They were standing near one of the benches and she sat on it, motioning him to join her.

"Whatever I call what is inside me, it is indissolubly connected with a certain young lady from China," said Professor Ferrier, seating himself close to her.

Had he said that? Yes, he had, and it was true. The effect Renfei had on him was that he could only tell her the truth. Where this was leading, he had no idea. He moved to tap his fingers on the bench, to get his thoughts in order, and then noticed her white knee. It occurred to him that if he touched it, it would mean that their relationship was no longer simply one of trust. He put his hand on her knee.

Renfei looked up quickly. She put an arm on his shoulder, pulled him toward her and kissed him on the lips. Then she sprang to her feet and walked away. He could not tell from her straight back and shoulders, and sturdy legs striding across the grass, whether she was angry or in a hurry.

15

LIYONG'S FACE WAS EVERYWHERE IN the media. He had suddenly returned to China, having been declared *persona non grata* by the Australian government and also disowned by China's ambassador in Canberra, a double negative that set chins wagging in informed political circles.

When the media first got wind of it, they had a field day: an agent of the Chinese government had been preying on young Chinese studying in Australia. Liyong got the treatment reserved for sports cheats and paedophiles, black headlines with words like "prey" and "lies" and "deceit" and a saturnine snapshot – slit eyes and a shifty look. This was bad China – a powerful country and culture that would not allow its people the freedom to live the way they wanted and was now scared that its young people, given the chance in Australia to think for themselves, would turn into opponents of the regime.

The vice-chancellor called a press conference. He chose a pin-line suit for the occasion and was pleased that it still fitted him. He was in good form, showing no sign of peevishness or paranoia, responding confidently to questions. "We nipped this assault on academic freedom in the bud." He assured the public that the university was alert to the dangers (as well as the opportunities) posed by a vast intake of international students. He accepted that campus security was his responsibility. It was a complex issue, impinging on the right of free inquiry. Fortunately, he had personally recently undertaken a rigorous review. The university had been able to act as soon as Liyong's presence became known.

In her interview, Andrea remained true to dogma's distant drum. Gillian tried hard to make her seem human, prefacing questions with "So how did it feel to ...? And "So what was it like when ...?" In desperation, she asked what everyone in the business community was asking: "And what is your view of the benefits for Australia in China's bright economic future?" Andrea was resolute, refusing to take the hint, determined to nail the boys in Beijing who had betrayed the revolution. Liyong's activities in Australia were a mere footnote to the bitter narrative of betrayal. The cameras did their best, closing on her saurian lower lip until it almost occupied the entire screen, catching the twitch of nervous fingers, but Andrea was indomitable. She had set her sights on the God that failed and nothing would prevent her from disembowelling it in public.

The Chinese ambassador called a press conference at his embassy in Canberra. Secure in a citadel of protocol, he gave a polished performance in impeccable English, with no trace of an American accent. He assured the Australian people that the Chinese government had "neither desire nor intention" of interfering with the relationship between teacher and student in Australian universities. What "transpired" in classrooms was a matter entirely for the "Australian authorities", he avowed, leaving open whether this meant the government or the universities. The Chinese embassy had been unaware of Mr Wang Liyong until his name was mentioned in a television program. The ambassador had been informed by the consulate in Melbourne that he had come to Australia in search of his childhood sweetheart, who was a student in Melbourne. To impress her, he had pretended to be a spy. The ambassador finessed a touch of humour. "Even young Chinese can occasionally be infected with the virus of James Bond." When question time arrived, he adopted a droll manner. Asked by a reporter if the Chinese government were cyber-spying on the Australian government, he disarmed the little gathering by saying, "I shall have to check with Beijing to see if we are yet abreast of our colleagues in the United States and Russia." Asked, "Is fear of China justified in Australia?" he responded like a weary doctor dealing with another outbreak of a preventible disease: sections of Australian society were "occasionally overcome by China-threat seizures". His final words were devoted to the "happy circumstance" that friendship between Australia and China was underpinned by "the economic imperative, which, as we all know, is basic to human progress."

After the ambassador's press conference, the media turned about, stampeding in the opposite direction. Liyong became a lovelorn lad who had given himself a romantic identity in order to win back the heart of his childhood sweetheart. He got the sexy boy-next-door treatment, words like "always" and "burning" and "yearning" in the headlines and pictures of a fresh-faced smiler (provided, without attribution, by the Melbourne consulate) with come-to-bed eyes. This was good China – the Chinese were human like everyone else. Moreover, China's vibrant economy was helping to keep Australia afloat in stormy global financial seas.

Gillian's opposition interviewed the childhood sweetheart's friend, Jian. He was almost as bad a subject, at the other end of the political spectrum, as Andrea. He scoffed at the suggestion that China was worried about its young people studying abroad. China's star was rising, while America's was setting. The vast enterprise of raising living standards in China was costly and demanding, so it was not possible to educate at home the entire next generation of Chinese leaders, but they would return equipped and committed to the task of taking the country to world leadership. China's youth were the "leading cadres", always ready for "combat at the front line"; they had never failed their country and would not fail it now. A new generation of leaders would return the country to the "vanguard of progressive thought". All he would say about Renfei was that she was "a nice, patriotic young woman". Unlike the United States, China was full of nice, patriotic young women.

"You know her well. Was Liyong right in his judgment of her, trying to impress her the way he did?"

Jian was a reincarnation of his mentor, the master diplomat Zhou Enlai, always on message. "Ms Liu Renfei is a nice, patriotic, young Chinese woman. I do not know Mr Wang Liyong, so I cannot speak of his intentions." He allowed himself only one rhetorical moment. Asked if he thought it was right or wrong for teachers to try to influence the political outlook of their students, he quoted Karl Marx. "As to rights and wrongs, the philosophers have only interpreted the world in various ways, the point is to change it." Faced with his impenetrable serenity, the interviewer gave up.

Everyone wanted to interview the childhood sweetheart herself. Renfei's student identity photograph had somehow found its way to the front page of a Melbourne newspaper, but it gave no hint of the qualities that had brought the lovelorn lad all the way from China. The media needed the real thing. "I've never seen the girl, but from all accounts she's stunning," Gillian had told a friend. This resonated around the networks, increasing the frenzy.

Gillian was incessantly on the phone to her father. "Apart from any personal connection, which I know you and that woman are unlikely to want to acknowledge publicly," she said, not just once, "it's only fair, considering all the work we've put into this story, that we should be the one to get an exclusive with that girl you've been harbouring. She is at the centre of it all, one way or another, a real main-chancer. She must have tipped off the Australian authorities. And she owes you. You've been good to her, plenty good. Free accommodation. Vonnie's car."

The guru listened. He could see Renfei on television, wearing one of those head-hugging hats that Mrs Winterbourne thought made her look thrilling. But he remained silent. He could not imagine Renfei tipping off anyone. "Thank you, dear girl," he would say at the end of a Gillian harangue, and then hang up.

Renfei parked the little red car in a side street and stayed at home. "The professor will understand," she told Lu, who wanted her to go to class "out of courtesy".

"You just want to be in the spotlight," Renfei said crossly.

"Why not?"

"You wouldn't want to be in the spotlight if you were going to be grilled by media persons on everything you do with your Jewish boyfriend."

"What about transparency? You should be helping." Lu was suddenly a responsible citizen.

"Transparency is meant for public life, not private."

"Public? Private? Who can be sure?"

Renfei felt alone. In the torrent of anger, intrigue and amusement released by the media, it was hard to know what was fact and what was fiction. She had lost her bearings; her feet were no longer on the ground. When she collected her wits, sat up straight and thought calmly, which was the way she usually pulled herself together, she faced a dilemma. She could not trust anyone. Not Lu or Jian or Knut, nor the professor, nor even Mr and Mrs Winterbourne. She had heard Australians say "They wanted his hide" and "They wanted a piece of him" and she had wondered what they meant. Now she knew. Everyone wanted a bit of her. They did not know what was inside her and even if they did, they didn't care. They just wanted little bits of her outside so they could say they knew what she was like.

Media people rang the doorbell and banged on the door, day and night. She crept under her bed. They set up cameras outside and waited. She could not play music nor listen to the radio until they had gone. She said rashly to Lu that if this was the way a free press operated, she would rather have it under government control.

"You should hire a manager," said Lu. "You can lay down the terms. The questions they are not allowed to ask. And how much they pay you for the interview."

"I just want to hide somewhere until it all blows over," Renfei said.

"Hiding makes people think you've done something wrong."

Renfei could not explain, even to Lu. She could not face the public with her mixed-up feelings about Liyong and Lijiang, the professor and the vice-chancellor. She could never explain to the television people the kind of life she wanted to live.

She rang home. Her sweet-faced parents were the same. The world's troubles passed them by, although times were tough, people without work were returning to their villages from the big cities, and crime was increasing. They were concerned about her. Was she getting good food, not staying up late, studying properly? She was almost at the end of her course. When would she be coming home?

Mrs Winterbourne rang to tell her that Johnno had reported that the "view in Canberra" was that China had been caught with its hand in the till. "I have spoken to the Morewitz and Burnside families," Mrs Winterbourne said, "and they wish you to know they are entirely on your side. Everyone thinks, of course, that Mr Winterbourne's daughter's television program is the pits." And hung up while Renfei was fumbling for a response.

One early morning, she put on her hooded coat and went for a walk. A mist clung to roofs and hedges and fog gathered in the dip in her street. She felt free and adventurous, striding off without direction while people were still inside their houses, some still sleeping. She could imagine them going through their morning routines, some cheerfully, some resentfully, some in a haze of uncertainty and anxiety, some purposeful and decisive. A dog barked. A child cried. A car's engine started. She passed a striding young woman stuffing high-heeled shoes into a backpack.

She noticed a small stone church with a sign outside: "This church is open for rest and prayer." She liked the invitation and went in. When she first came to Australia, churches were forbidden territory. She was the only person in the church. On a table at the entrance was a placard appealing for funds for Christians in the Middle East; the faithful were being driven out of the Holy Land by poverty and bloody persecution. Aid was urgently needed for refugees and to rebuild churches and convents. A crucifix of olive wood, handcrafted in Bethlehem, would be sent to anyone who gave a donation of $20 or more. She walked down a red carpet between rows of pews and took a seat in the middle. She had noticed the church because of its windows, delicate blue emblems on a lime background. From inside, with the sunlight coming through, they were translucent. The interior was simple, cream walls rising to dark wood panelling and rafters. A huge wooden cross, with a lifelike Christ figure on it, stood over an altar with a faded purple cloth. She breathed deeply; she imagined the air was pure, uncontaminated by desires and fears and ambitions outside. She remembered what she had been told at school about religion, the "opium of the people". Still, she wondered, perhaps it was necessary to allow religious freedom so that people who were religious could live freely, just as you might allow homosexuals to be themselves, not because you approved or wanted everyone to be homosexual, but because to suppress the right to be one was to endanger freedom in general?

The danger was even greater with religion, because it claimed to know the answers to all those questions that everyone kept asking, like how the universe was created and what happened when you died. It could be argued (as the professor had when she had asked him about the soul) that human rights, including religious freedom, were a legal, political and social fact that the otherwise all-powerful state could be forced by law to accept, but religion had a special place in people's lives. It was more challenging than any of the other freedoms, because it asked you to believe in a power beyond earthly power, including the power of those running the state. Was it therefore a necessary condition of true freedom?

Renfei thought of her parents in sleepy Lijiang. They were just two people, with a wayward daughter in Australia, coping with what the authorities in Beijing decided was good for them. They were part of the great civilisation that was China, but they had no say in what was happening in China, like Tiger Leaping Gorge, gouging the landscape nearby; they just learned how to live with it.

She could see her father, easing his toes from his sandals to catch the sun while reading the newspaper on the front porch. He would glance up now and then and look steadily at the line of distant blue hills. Was he checking the weather? Or taking comfort from the fact that the hills were always there, unchanged? He was dressed in a quilted jacket. He always took care of his appearance, not, you felt, because of vanity but out of respect for social order. He believed you should dress properly in public, as you expected others to dress – if you didn't, society looked ragged. If it looked ragged, those who wanted to turn it upside down were encouraged. He had come to Lijiang when they were married because he wanted to be a "barefoot doctor", looking after people who lived far from the amenities of the big cities. She could see her mother, busy in the kitchen. She missed the social excitement of city life. She did not understand her husband's commitment to rural people. If he wanted to help the poor, there were just as many poor people in cities. She did not complain. She had tried to get him to go back to the city, pointing out the opportunities during China's economic boom when the cities were flooded with rural migrants, but he always found an excuse to stay.

She thought of Liyong and the twists and turns of government service. Nations were all different but the state was more or less the same. It had the right to do things that no one else could, and it had the means, especially the police and the armed forces. International organisations and institutions, like the United Nations, were trying to establish rules for everyone. The professor believed that for the world to be peaceful and prosperous the nations had to give up their sovereign rights and cooperate with each other to strengthen the rules. Sitting quietly in the church, Renfei asked herself if religion might help. It was peaceful, having no armed forces. It sought moral authority to humble the state, preventing it from thinking it could do whatever it liked.

She could hear Lu's laughter. All the religions were founded and run by men. The state, for all its faults, had accepted women as equal with men in politics, business, professions, the arts and journalism, but religion held on to the notion that, as God was a man, women were inferior. How could any movement that excluded half the population of the world from its leadership be useful? She laughed out loud, recalling stern-faced men solemnly pronouncing on something they knew nothing about – sex.

Renfei folded her hands and rubbed her toes together, raising her eyes to gold-leafed candelabra hanging from the rafters. She had seen a quotation from Oscar Wilde posted in Federation Square: "Life is too important to be taken seriously." She constructed a humorous sentence in her head. "Religion should be tolerated because empty churches are a quiet space for troubled souls."

She rose decorously, nodded in salutation to the Christ figure on the cross, walked down the aisle of red carpet, placed a small coin in the box for the persecuted faithful in the Holy Land and strode into the sunshine.

A letter from Liyong arrived in the morning mail. She examined the local postmark; it was sent before he left. She unfolded the large page with trembling fingers. It was calligraphy in the old style, characters both bold and fragile, reminding her of cliffs around Lijiang that towered and hung dangerously at the same time. It was not really a letter. It was a proclamation, telling her that he was right and she was wrong.

"Civilisation depends on authority, including the use of force. Only the impotent are pure. There are no human rights in countries where the state fails and order collapses."

That was all. It was imperious, untroubled by ifs and buts. She could see his eyebrows rising and falling as he delicately formed the characters, finishing with a flourish. She sat with the page in her hand, reliving what she had done.

She had rejected Liyong, so she had had to reject the professor as well. If she didn't, it would mean that she had rejected China in favour of Australia. It could even mean that she had decided to settle in Australia. Neither of these were true or at least (remembering Freud) she had not consciously decided to reject China in favour of Australia, nor to leave China and live in Australia. And there was something else. She would have been betraying her friends, whether she passed on what they said in moments of intimacy outside the classroom or in discussion inside the classroom. The likely consequences were more drastic in one case than the other, but she had no control over them either way. The issue for her was not the greater good nor the national interest, neither liberty nor order, but what was inside her. In neither situation would she be true to herself.

She had made her decision. Now she had to live with it.

16

THEY SET OUT EARLY. RENFEI was keen to escape from the fishbowl that Liyong had dropped her in and was also uncertain also whether the little red car was up to the task. Mr Westbourne's Pacific Ocean was a mythical place, even with his map and precise directions. She was anxious about the little car's roadworthiness, anxious about her driving ability, anxious whether they had brought the right baggage, anxious about telling Lu of the car's former owner. She kept tapping the fuel gauge on the dashboard, as if the "full" sign were not believable, although she assured Lu several times that the tank was "brimmed to its utmost". She was anxious about the booking Mr Winterbourne had made for them at The Black Dolphin. She was anxious about getting back in time for the last class of the semester. She had carefully calculated the mileage on Mr Winterbourne's map and allowed them to be away two nights and three days.

"One double bed," she said abruptly, as they drove through Dandenong, reminding herself of the booking at The Black Dolphin. They were used to sleeping together.

"Will there be sharks or crocodiles?" Lu had asked when Renfei had said they would be "voyaging" to the Pacific Ocean. "There are always sharks or crocodiles on Australian holidays."

She was given the role of navigator, assisted by detailed notes compiled by Mr Winterbourne. The little car nosed its way competently through Drouin and headed for Warragul. "Warra Gull," announced Lu, giving it a Chinese flavour. "War of the gulls!" she interpreted freely. She admired the scenery, green pastures sloping up on one side to small blue hills. Examining the guru's road map, she murmured wonderingly, "Alpine road?"

She announced all the road signs. "Keep in Left Lane Unless Overtaking."

Renfei was not thinking of overtaking anyone. Sleek cars and trucks like railway carriages marked "Long Vehicle" rushed past the little red car, which was as far left as she could keep it without making a squealing noise on the marker line.

She was troubled by the legacy of Veronica. The sadness, not just of her death but of the effect it must have had on Mr Winterbourne, impregnated the little red car. Everything had happened in such a hurry that she had not had time to tell Lu. Or, she had had the time but not the inclination. She knew Lu would make fun of it and she knew that Mr Winterbourne was intense about it; she felt she would be exposing him unfairly. She had felt confident before, a gift had passed from one to another without encumbrance. Now it had a life of its own and she was not sure, as she sat at the driving wheel and pointed the car's nose towards the Pacific Ocean, whether it would obey her as readily as it did before.

"Drowsy Drivers Die!" Lu announced.

They skirted Warragul and, according to the guru's notes, set off for the brown coal world of open cut mining that had once made Victoria the proud host of the cheapest electricity in the world, and was now depressed and dirty.

"The dirtiest power station in the industrialised world," Lu read. "You can see the smoke stacks, belching out their poison."

"There's something I have to tell you," Renfei said, as more smoke stacks came into view.

"Eyes Open? Sleep Can Kill!"

"Lu, be sensible. There's something I need to say."

"Historic Marker! 300 metres on Left."

"Lu!"

"You told me to keep my eyes open."

Renfei could not decide whether she should gently steer the little car into the next parking space or just shout above the noise of the engine, displaced air and Lu's dramatic commentary. She did neither, deciding that the first would be melodramatic and the second difficult.

"What do you need to tell me?"

"Nothing. It can wait."

"Can't Concentrate? Take a Powernap!"

The countryside rolled away from them, green and inviting despite the gloomy smoke stacks and Mr Winterbourne's notes on climate change. He advised that if they had to make a stop, they should take care to lock the car doors and not open their wallets in front of anyone.

"He's cranky," said Lu.

"He is informed well about many things," said Renfei.

"Yes. But the question is whether he's off his head." Renfei would not be drawn into saying anything bad about Mr Winterbourne. "He's with the birds," said Lu. "Like the professor. Only worse."

Renfei kept her opinion to herself. Lu could not be expected to know about "wayward persons".

"Only Sleep Cures Fatigue," Lu declared. And: "A Microsleep Can Kill in Seconds!"

She slouched in her seat. "I'm confused. Is sleep good or bad?"

In Sale, described by the guru as "gracious and old-fashioned", they stopped for coffee and, rejuvenated, set out for Bairnsdale, which they were informed was "bustling, the commercial centre of Gippsland", and Lakes Entrance, where they would see the end of the Ninety Mile Beach.

"How much is that in kilometres?" Lu asked.

The coffee shop in Sale had been so sedate and quiet that Renfei had been too scared to speak about Veronica. Now, on the road again, she was busy driving and coping with Lu's announcements. And there was something about the road itself that absorbed her, the idea of a road map, with destinations that were little destinies beyond your control, yet there on a map, with distances carefully marked, available if you just kept driving at a certain speed for a certain time.

It was comforting having everything laid out for you. She could hear the professor: "Freedom is not anarchy. When the state fails, when there is no order, the result is anarchy, not freedom." The air rushed past. She wished the little red car had one of those roofs that folded back, so she and Lu could have the air in their faces.

They swept through Stratford, on the river Avon. "As in England," said Lu, consulting her notes. Except that the river was dry.

"Feeling Drowsy? Take a Powernap."

"What is the difference between a nap and a powernap?" Lu asked.

Compared with the bustling commercial centres of China, Bairnsdale was as composed as Sale and they pressed on to Lakes Entrance to see the beach, whose length in kilometres Lu was still working out. A roadside lookout was thoughtfully provided, with binoculars, but when all was said and done, as Renfei remarked, the idea of a long beach was more interesting than the reality. When you examined the patch of it within your own range, it was much the same as anywhere else. They reserved judgment, out of respect for the guru, and pressed on.

Renfei kept looking at her watch. She planned to be at The Black Dolphin before nightfall. She was worried that they would be stuck somewhere on the vast Australian coast in the dark, so she "brimmed up" the little car's petrol tank.

"A Fifteen Minute Powernap Can Save Your Life!" announced Lu on the way to Orbost. "It makes you drowsy thinking about it."

Renfei played her favourite disk, Yo-Yo Ma, with piano and clarinet (and a Portuguese songstress), which she knew took an hour and would take them beyond Orbost and on the way to Cann River. From there they would visit Point Hicks, which provided Captain Cook with his first glimpse of Australia. At the fourth selection, in which the cello and the clarinet combined to produce sounds of sweet and unattainable yearning, she told Lu about Veronica.

Lu listened without responding. Renfei turned off Yo-Yo Ma and the silence was so lengthy that she felt the need to break it herself. "I think Mr Winterbourne is still in grief."

Lu shifted uneasily in her seat and glanced over her shoulder at the back of the car.

"Did she kill herself in the car?"

Renfei explained how Veronica had been found lying on her side by a creek.

"Well, that's something," said Lu.

The intensity of traffic signs had subsided, the traffic was light and the trees, banked on either side of the road, gave a feeling of sepulchral seclusion to the little car bent on its fanciful mission to the Pacific Ocean. Lu seemed stuck for something to say. There were some things that even she could not make fun of. Then a traffic accident sign appeared.

"Death Is So Long," she announced, recovering confidence.

"They say spirits can only travel in a straight line," she announced. "Chinese don't go in a straight line. We zigzag, not even zigzag, more like little steps backward and forward, sideways, up and down. So we are safe from evil spirits."

She took the matter further. "We adapt and move on. I can sleep anywhere. My boyfriend can't sleep unless everything is right, the mattress, the right time, no worries. I don't worry about anything. Even exams. It's just another bit of life and you take it on, do it."

Renfei turned on Yo-Yo Ma again and his music filled the little car with the pleasure of longing.

At Cann River, a crossroads between the Snowy Mountains to the north and inhospitable coastal terrain to the south, they were duty-bound to turn south. The guru had written: "The great Cook first sighted Australia on 19 April 1770 in latitude 38 degrees. Actually, a Dutchman, Abel Janszoon Tasman, sailing from Batavia in 1642 had already traced the western coastline of Australia and had landed on the west coast of Tasmania. The Dutch, sailing around the Cape of Good Hope to the East Indies, were sometimes blown off course to land on the western coast of Australia, but they did not like it – the coast was barren and dangerous and the inhabitants were savage, black and had nothing to trade. Cook was the only one to come to Australia from the Pacific and he was the only one to lay claim to it. But he decided not to land at Point Hicks and proceeded up the coast to Botany Bay (Sydney)."

The two Chinese girls studied the guru's note carefully. The road map said 16 kms to a dispersal juncture, leading to a lighthouse and other features. Add another five kilometres. But the sign at Cann River said 45 kilometres. Lu advised that Point Hicks was noted not just for its light station (not a lighthouse) but also for snorkelling, walking on dunes and observing an assortment of 52 mammal species, 26 reptile species and 306 species of birds.

"Should we bother?" Renfei was looking at her watch again.

"Let's give it a go." Lu was in reckless mood.

But the prospect was not inviting. The little car wound its way over a landscape of scrub on a dirt road, corrugated and potholed, without traffic directions or any sign of life. Also, it began to rain. After half an hour, Renfei pulled over. It occurred to her that the signpost saying 45 kilometres was a discreet way of saying there was no human habitation when you got there. No café. No petrol. You had to come back. If you could!

"What do you think?"

"The cook knew," said Lu. "He went north."

They turned back and headed for Twofold Bay and the entrance to what the guru declared was the "fabled embrace" of the Pacific Ocean, leaving the cold waters of the Tasman Sea behind them.

"Australian history is new," said Renfei, as if what they had missed did not matter anyway.

"The road needs an upgrade," said Lu.

"The authorities do not want people to know where the cook first saw Australia," Renfei agreed. "You would expect at least an info bureau."

The little car took valiantly to the road for the last stretch of their journey to the Pacific. "If the Tas Man had claimed Australia, all this would be Dutch," said Lu, waving at forests, delighted at how simple it was to overturn history. "And there would be no Union Jack on the flag. My Jewish boyfriend is in favour of a republic."

"The British did a good job and now the Australians are taking over." Renfei was protective of the professor and his family.

"China should invade and give them more history than the British. Or the Dutch."

"Lu! You sound like Jian."

"Jian says no one could stop us. The Americans are bankrupt. We own their treasury bills, whatever they are. The Japanese might try to stop us. More likely, Jian says, they will invade Taiwan, so we will have to go to war with them to save the Kuomintang!" Lu chuckled at the irony. "The British were clever in Australia. They put all the main ports and cities in the south, so any invader from the north would have to cross all that desert. Whose side would the Aborigines be on?"

Renfei declined with a toss of her head to acknowledge that this was a serious question, but Lu, or her boyfriend, had been giving it some thought. "He says the Aborigines would welcome an invader. They have been treated like shit, even when they signed up to fight with the Australian forces in the Second World War against the Japanese."

"Like the Tibetans and the Uighurs," said Renfei. "Whose side would they be on?"

"Good question."

It was a question that remained unanswered as the little red car quietly digested the distance separating them from their destiny. While they were still on the outskirts of Eden, they were startled by glimpses of the brilliant blue of the Pacific Ocean. Lu read from a brochure the guru had provided.

"Is there another colour that can simultaneously soothe and excite your senses the way blue does? Does any other colour have so many names? Cobalt. Navy. Powder. Indigo. Royal. Prussian. Midnight. Ultramarine. Azure. It is everywhere, above and below, and all around you, constantly reflected by a million mirrors, flowing, lapping, bubbling, shining, swelling, rising and falling."

"Good advertising copy," said Renfei. But it was true, the blue seemed to be everywhere, after the green of their journey. Even the trees were affected. Silvery ghost gums stood off in the distance like sentinels.

Lu wanted to go whale watching but Renfei looked steadily at her watch. "We must press on." She had her mind on Merimbula. Not until they were safely bedded down in The Black Dolphin would she be confident that they had reached the objective of the journey the guru of the Pacific had devised for them.

They ran along the windswept shore. The sand was as white as salt. The wind whipped the dry part of the beach into a veil of flying sand, stinging their legs. They were the only people on the beach and they scampered like children, laughing back at their footprints in the wet sand.

"We are the only people in the world!" Lu shouted.

It was early morning in Merimbula, after a good night's sleep at The Black Dolphin, and before breakfast, which Renfei promised would be "heartful". She had examined the menu and decided that for financial and dietary reasons, as well as its European flavour, the continental selection would be adequate. Hearty Australian breakfasts were not appropriate for young Chinese women. She had taken charge of the budget for both of them. Petrol was expensive. And paying to sleep in a bed when they had their own perfectly good bed empty in Melbourne offended some deep sense of propriety.

She ran to the water's edge and cupped a handful against her lips. "The Pacific Ocean has a bountiful taste."

She became aware of something in the sky, too large for a bird; it caught the glow of the early sun, and she could see that it was attached to a line. It must be a kite, even if it looked like a drone or a parachute. The way it kicked and jumped and slid in the wind made her think there must be someone on the beach tugging it, but she could not see anyone. The beach was a short walk from the motel, past some new holiday units with names like Sea Breeze and Pacific View, through a sandy strip of ti-tree. She looked back to the seafront balconies for the kite's controller. But Merimbula was still sleeping. Then she saw a figure see-sawing on waves out at sea.

"We are not alone," she said to Lu.

She watched as the man (she was sure it was a man, although the gender could not be detected in the dip and splash of the waves) battled with the elements. He was riding a board, legs bent at the knees and quickly reversible, arms thrust stiffly out in front, as is he were steering a motorbike, although she could now see he was gripping a stick attached to the kite's line. At times it seemed all he could do was stop himself from being lifted into the air (taken off, she fancied, to some mountain fastness). Yet he was able to manipulate the kite while surfing on the board, heading back out to sea to catch the next wave, then swooping in curves that brought the kite lower and lower, each time bringing him closer to shore. She could see now that he was a man, a boy perhaps, tall and slender. Eventually he swooped wider and wider in a circle that brought him into shallow water, where he jumped from the board and tucked it under one arm.

Then he was standing on their beach, hauling in the kite. He flashed a wide grin in their direction. He seemed to be saying something that could not be heard against the wind, so they approached him. He was an Australian Aborigine.

"That fella plenty boisterous," he said, indicating the kite, now lost behind a clump of bushes. He was wearing only a pair of shorts and his black body glistened in the morning sun. His voice had a lift and a lilt that appealed to Renfei; she savoured his use of "boisterous".

"How does it work?" asked Lu.

The boy seemed mystified by the need to explain something that was obvious. "Just hold on," he said cheerfully. "When that jumbuck gets going." He flicked the line in the hope of landing the kite, which proved successful, and he pulled at it gently, like landing a fish. "Where you from?"

It was one of those abrupt Australian questions, Renfei thought, that could mean anything. Up the road? The Black Dolphin? Melbourne? China? "China," she said.

"Go on." You could not tell whether he was impressed or incredulous. "Lijiang," she said. He nodded, as if Lijiang was personally known to him and regarded with indifference.

"I'm from Beijing, where the Olympics were held," said Lu with a toss of her head. She wasn't from Beijing; she had only been there for university as Renfei had been in Shanghai, but that was Lu.

"Yeah," said the boy, with the same nod of impenetrable acceptance.

"You live around here?" asked Renfei. She noticed that her voice had slipped into a laconic style like the boy's. He jerked a finger over his shoulder in a direction that could lead anywhere, scarcely interrupting his careful recovery of the kite.

"Time for breakfast," said Lu. "I'm hungry."

"Yeah," said the boy.

On their way back to The Black Dolphin, Lu wondered whether she should have mentioned breakfast. "He is quite thin." She pondered. "My Jewish boyfriend says they live on witchetty grubs." Lu always referred to her boyfriend as "Jewish". She thought that if she just said "boyfriend" people would assume he was Chinese. "Why don't you just say Australian boyfriend. He's not religious, is he?" Renfei asked.

"I don't think of him as Australian. He's like a European."

"That one we just met was a real Australian," said Renfei. "The first Aboriginal person I've met since I came to Australia." She smiled. "New experience."

"He was good looking, in his own way," said Lu.

"What age do you think he is?"

"Eighteen." Lu considered. "Younger than us."

"He was strong on that board." Renfei seemed to be considering the possibility that he might be older.

"It's hard to tell with them," said Lu. "They're different."

During breakfast which, to Lu's delight, was delivered on time to their room, they discussed their itinerary. They would visit Tathra, the prettiest spot on the so-called Sapphire Coast (in the guru's opinion), drive along the edge of the iconic Pacific Ocean to Bermagui, observe Mt Dromedary, sighted and named by the great Cook because its outline reminded him of a camel, then ... well, it was up to them. They had reached the shores of the fabled Pacific, run along its white sands, breathed its healthy air.

"We haven't yet bathed in the sacred waters," said Renfei. Her voice was free of irony. "Perhaps this is a good place to do it."

They had brought swimming gear and examined themselves in the mirror, Lu flouncing in a pink bikini, Renfei solemn in a costume of mottled grey. Check-out was 10 am. There was time. The wind was cool but the sun was shining.

"I forgot to bring a hat." Renfei's sensitive skin and aversion to beach behaviour had to be accommodated. "Do you think reception provides umbrellas?"

Lu was ready to go. "Hold a towel over your head. We don't need to stay long, just a dip to make the old crank happy."

"Are we allowed to take towels from the room?"

"Just take them. Who will know? We'll only be away ten minutes."

So they returned to the brilliantly white beach, stepping gingerly in sandalled heels through the ti-tree strip, Renfei in a white bathrobe, Lu in a striped blue housecoat, towels held over their heads. They disrobed and entered the water on pale and sturdy legs, towels aloft.

"We don't need to get our heads wet," said Renfei. "Just a dip."

The wind had dropped, no longer whipping up a veil of stinging sand, but the beach was still barely occupied. A couple of boys were bodysurfing and a family of four had come prepared to settle in for the day, equipped with beach umbrellas, deck chairs and eskies. An elderly couple in shorts strode quickly past.

"Power walkers," said Lu.

They subsided into the water up to their necks, kneeling, and then decorously seating themselves. The effort of shielding themselves from the sun with overhead towels affected their stability; they smiled gamely at each other as they wobbled above lapping wavelets.

Then Renfei saw the boy. He was lounging on the sand with his head propped in one hand. She shouted: "Look at us!" In her head, she added: "Chinese girls up to our necks in your Pacific Ocean!" He swivelled on his elbow, rising in a movement that was neither standing nor walking, a bit of both. Then he was stalking towards them.

He stood at the water's edge looking down on their bobbing heads under the towels. "What's the towels for?"

"Keeping the sun from our faces," shouted Renfei. "We forgot to bring hats."

His expression drifted from curiosity to wonder. He had not encountered such prophylactic delicacy before. "What's your name?" They told him, bobbing up and down, their modest bodies covered by the sacred water. "What's yours?"

"Gubaga," he said, then shrugged. "You can call me Jimmy, if you want." He said "if you want" more as a rebuff than an invitation.

"I like Gubaga," said Lu. "Gu Ba Ga. It's like Yo Yo Ma. And O Ba Ma. The world is becoming Chinese!"

"My great grandma was Chinese," he said.

The two girls stopped bobbing. They both looked at the boy, his thin black body, his deep-set eyes, his long face, his cadaverous head, his hair with a hint of curls.

"What was her name?" Lu was quick to grasp essentials.

"Annie Hoy. They met on the goldfields." The boy knew what he was talking about. "You been to Tilba Tilba?"

The girls rose as one, shaking their heads, emerging slowly from the Pacific Ocean. Renfei transferred her towel to her body, Lu threw hers over one shoulder and stood in front of Gubaga with a hand on a hip.

"So you're Chinese!"

"You reckon." The boy reckoned otherwise. "Chinese don't like the sun." His taut, flippant manner was automatic, as if it were expected of him.

Renfei felt obliged to explain. "Australian sun is bad for your skin if you are not used to it."

"Yeah, I heard." He was a different embodiment of the human species, from whose skin the sun bounced harmlessly away.

"You come from here?" asked Lu.

"Up the coast. You tourists?"

"We're students. In Melbourne."

"What you doing here?"

They both realised that to give an honest answer that the boy could also understand was impossible, so Renfei just said, "Taking a break from studies."

He nodded in his impersonal way. "Good place for a break." Then, as if obliged to issue a formal qualification, "If you're not a black bastard like me." Renfei and Lu heard the words and understood them well enough to check any quick response, but were still unsure how to proceed.

"I'm a student," said the boy.

"What are you studying?" Renfei asked.

"Mickey Mouse stuff." He twisted his lips. "You doing accountancy?"

As neither of them were, Renfei regained her interest in Gubaga, or perhaps Jimmy. "What makes you think we would do accountancy?"

"Foreigners get points for immigration." Stated in his strangely elegant, impassive fashion, it was not a criticism.

"Black bastards don't need immigration points," said Lu. They all burst into laughter at that.

"Yeah," said Gubaga. "I'm part of the scenery."

Yes, Renfei thought, you are. But not part of the holiday scenery, the smart new houses and motels near the beach and estuary and the apartment blocks rearing on Merimbula's high ground, seeking a glimpse of Pacific blue. He was part of the sea itself and the trees and mountains in the distance.

"We are going to see Mt Dromedary."

"Gulaga Mountain," said Gubaga. "Belongs to Yuin nation."

He stretched his long body, arms above his head, and yawned.

"Take a powernap!" said Lu.

The two girls put their hands over their mouths and giggled. Gubaga gave a broad, uncomprehending grin.

"I could do with a cuppa something."

He prepared to wander off, stating his need as if it were a matter of indifference to him and anyone who heard him. He had changed his clothes and was now wearing a khaki shirt and faded jeans, but his feet were still bare. He had rid himself of the parachute kite.

"They've got tea and biscuits in the rooms at The Black Dolphin," said Lu, directing the information to Renfei, who turned inquiringly to the boy.

"I'll be in it," he said, setting off in the motel's direction.

At The Black Dolphin, the girls packed the car and Renfei paid at the office, while Gubaga had two cups of tea and four biscuits.

"Very nice," Renfei said, when asked for her impression of the motel and its service. She hurried back to their room, threatened by the irrational fear that Lu and Gubaga should not be left alone together. She sensed that Lu was not sympathetic to the boy's languid style and might say something foolish, or even racist. But they were laughing together, waiting for her at the car, ready to go.

The three musketeers (nominated by Renfei recalling her literary studies at Tongji university) drove in the little red car along the guru's beloved Pacific coast, Gubaga in the front passenger seat, so that he could display his local knowledge, and Lu in the back, where she was prevented from commenting on road signage. She had brought her laptop and was intent on reading her e-mail.

Gubaga did not say where he was living, nor where he expected to return when they parted. He explained in his gruff, lilting voice that he was a member of the Yuin nation, the original owners of the lands and waters from Merimbula to Sydney and inland to the mountains (the Great

Dividing Range, in whitefella lingo). His people had been there long before Captain Cook sailed up the coast and claimed everything for the British.

"Yuin sounds Chinese," said Renfei. "Yu In. Like Yu Jin, the famous general in the Three Kingdoms period."

"Go on," said Gubaga. "How old is that?"

"Maybe two thousand years ago." Renfei wrinkled her forehead.

"Yeah. We've been here longer than that." He looked across at the driver's profile. "You think it sounds Chinese?" He seemed pleased.

"If you google Yuin nation you get Yu Jin," Lu announced, head down in the back seat. "And premier Yu declaring the independence of the nation of Taiwan."

"Taiwan is not a nation," said Renfei.

"Yeah," said the boy. "Whitefellas don't think Yuin is a nation." He was surly, but not unsociable. Renfei noticed his hand, with piano player's fingers. She had left her flute in Melbourne.

Lu informed the front seat: "The Yuin population was about 11,000 when Cook first sighted them from his ship, the *Endeavour*. Now it's just a few hundred."

"Yeah." The Yuin nation's representative confirmed the bleak picture. "Just about wiped out."

The coast rolled past on the driver's side and Renfei dreamed of Captain Cook in braided uniform and spyglass on his little wooden ship, searching the shore anxiously for somewhere to land safely while Gubaga's ancestors hid behind rocks and trees with spears at the ready. It was different in China. People were the same, even thousands of years earlier. There were poor people with barely enough to live and rich people who wore elaborate clothes and jewellery and built themselves mansions and palaces, but culturally they were the same. The tension between them was the same as the tension between rich and poor in China now. Human emotions were the same now as then – jealousy and love and hate and anger, all recorded in official documents and letters and literature. But the early Australians were like a race apart, like the kangaroos and koalas.

"What did your people think when they saw the cook's ship?" asked Lu.

Gubaga swayed his head from side to side as if considering several possibilities, or perhaps just teasing out a single hypothesis. "Curious." He was matter-of-fact. "They'd heard stories of people from other lands." He spoke over his shoulder, addressing Lu. "We been here a long time. People keep coming." But he didn't speak with confidence. Renfei suspected that he did not know what the Yuin people thought when Captain Cook sailed up the coast. Did they actually see them? They didn't have telescopes like the captain. When Cook landed at Botany Bay the local people there would know and word would get around, but how long would it take for Gubaga's people to find out? And by the time the story got to them, it would be garbled.

"Why didn't the cook land here?" Lu exclaimed at the sweep of the bay, when they got their first sight of Tathra. Gubaga took them to the old wharf, where there was a museum. Renfei declared there were two kinds of history, one with relics you could touch and see (like the old wharf and the museum) and the other in the air, like the wind in the trees. Gubaga was pleased with her, nodding slowly as she spoke. "You'll see when we get to Tilba."

At Wapengo, they skirted the estuary to the accompaniment of Yo-Yo Ma, observing silently the stands of stately ghost gums at water's edge. Renfei said it felt sad. Gubaga said "the whole lot of it" was sad, then regaled them with tales of the fishing prowess of the Yuin nation. He jiggled his shoulders to the music, mouthing the name of the American president.

At Bermagui he drew their attention to Gulaga Mountain, looming inland. The "ancestral origin of the Yuin people" and "the basis of their spiritual identity" announced Lu in a voice strained with unaccustomed dignity.

"Yeah." He grinned at Renfei, man of the world. "A few years back freehold title to the mountain was given to us by the government up the coast in Sydney."

The little car found its way through winding country lanes, green pastures and grazing fat cattle to a small, prefabricated and intensely manicured village in the shadow of the mountain. This was Tilba, a National Trust village described in a declaration, Lu informed the front seat, as "175 years of living history" after alluvial and reef gold had been discovered on Mt Dromedary.

"Relic history," said Renfei.

"Instant history," said Lu. "They have to change the sign every year."

"Yeah." He was pleased to have his view of Tilba confirmed. "Nothing blowing in the wind here," he said to Renfei.

They parked in the space allotted to parking and strolled into a street of wooden shops and houses, some dating back to the late 19th century, some recently built in the style of the original. Two young Chinese women and a young Aboriginal man were an unusual sight. The busy pedestrian traffic was otherwise Caucasian, of middle and later ages, some with children or grandchildren. They were all wearing the casual clothes of retirement or tourism and the expressions of people who had discovered a gem in the desert of ordinary life and were determined to enjoy their good fortune. They juggled ice-creams and saveloys and cups of tea and sandwiches, bit into hot new bread, darted in and out of gift shops to look at ancient pieces of clothing and artefacts in the natural light, and examined the names on the war memorial. They sniffed at Tilba's famous cheeses, lingered under rose-covered arbours, played old gramophone records and turned over second-hand books.

It was time for lunch. Renfei could see no Chinese food on offer and was unsure whether Gubaga paid for himself or had somehow become her responsibility. His jeans fitted him like a glove and she could not see where he might carry a wallet. Remembering Ye Olde Curiosity Shoppe, she wondered aloud if they might have Devonshire tea.

Outside Pam's Store, Gubaga explained they could trek to the top of Gulaga Mountain and back in four hours. A track that began behind the store would show them the way.

"I would rather have Devonshire tea," said Lu.

So it was over Devonshire tea that he told them of his great plan to save Australia and the world. He dropped his laconic style and became eloquent. He was studying environmental law, which was the closest he could get to what he considered was the key to the future of the human race. He was amused by what whitefellas thought was the "big picture" and many young blackfellas were copying. Macroeconomics! His lip curled. Globalisation! Sociology and political culture! A waste of time.

A Young Woman From China

The really big picture was all that energy swirling around up there in the universe and its effect on the spiritual connection between human beings and other forms of life on earth. If you could tap into that, you had the game won. Radicals of both white and black variety thought the answer was to get indigenous people to adapt to industrial society – learn how to live in cities, learn a trade, compete for jobs that society needed, adopt a social culture that explained everything in terms of production and consumption. Some Australian blackfellas were playing the whitefella's game by protest marching, demanding land rights and getting caught up in legal battles. But the blackfella knew in his bones that this was not the way. This was just a distraction. The big picture was the harmony of all that energy out there in the universe and the harmony of life, flora and fauna, on the surface of the earth. And the whitefella was starting to catch on.

"He knows he's got to change course," said Gubaga, his fingers covered in strawberry jam and cream. "He's got the science in his head. What he doesn't know is that the blackfella's got the answer in his bones. In our genes, like they say now." He gave a broad grin. "We got it on the tip of our tongue. Give us the science and we'll give you the answer."

"Are Chinese whitefellas?" asked Lu.

"You are," said Gubaga. "You're scared of the sun."

He would continue to study environmental law but he was interested in astronomy. It made sense that all that energy up there was controlled by planets and stars in their different orbits, and galaxies swirling around, just like the sea had currents and winds. It must have an effect on the universe, including planet earth. Aborigines thought of the earth as their mother. It took care of you, so you took care of it.

"We been watching and thinking for a long time. We don't write it down like the whitefella but it's in our heads, in stories, and now blackfella artists are telling these stories to the world."

Gubaga sat back in his chair. He had reached a point in his narrative that required him to look each of his companions in the eye, both of them, one after the other.

"I want to be an artist of the universe," he said.

Renfei smiled. An Australian in her international business class was always talking about being "master of the universe". The other Australians thought he had "tickets on himself". She wondered about Gubaga. But he was not as visionary as he seemed. He explained that blackfellas were not much good at whitefella stuff, like learning a trade, but they were good at singing and dancing. He would have a song and dance show on television, which would give him the chance to speak some blackfella wisdom, like the whitefella television people did.

Lu was enthusiastic. His program could be called Aboriginal Idol!

Renfei had been glancing at her watch for some time. She had calculated that either they would stay that night at a nearby motel, probably in Bermagui or Bega, or they could try to get closer to Melbourne, reducing the distance of the home run the next day. She was concerned that the little red car might find all the activity too much.

Gubaga saved her the trouble of asking. "I'd better be getting along."

"Can we take you somewhere?"

"Up the road to the Umbarra cultural centre."

When they arrived, the gate was closed and padlocked with a chain. A sign overhead said Visitors Welcome. Gubaga got out of the car to read a handwritten notice on the gate. He shrugged. "Today visitors not welcome." He climbed over the barred gate and sauntered up the gravel road, turning to wave a diffident farewell, his hand not high in the sky but low, near his knee. Then he grinned and cupped his ear. Listening to the wind!

They discussed their new Australian experience all the way to Bombala. They were returning to Melbourne not just with a taste of the Pacific Ocean but with a whiff of old Australia. Renfei thought Gubaga was shy and was surprised that he had exposed his inner thoughts to them.

"He's like me," she said. "He's got something inside he has to get out."

Lu wasn't sure about Gubaga. "My boyfriend says they can live on the smell of an oily rag."

"How could that be?" Renfei was puzzled.

"It's an Australian joke," said Lu.

17

AT PROFESSOR FERRIER'S LAST CLASS for the semester, he would reveal the winner of a valuable scholarship that was established to assist a foreign student to proceed to a doctorate. It was a university award, normally announced by the vice-chancellor who had agreed, however, that because the winner this year was in the professor's class, he could disclose it informally an hour before the vice-chancellor's office made the official announcement.

"For services rendered, Ian," the vice said, with a knowing look that the professor found distasteful. He did not want to be reminded of his role in the Liyong fiasco.

Lu arrived early and sat in the middle of the front row, saving seats for Renfei, Jian and Knut. The room filled rapidly. Word had got around that the spy thriller's leading lady would be present.

"Where is she?" the Chinese girls asked Lu, one after the other, when Jian and Knut had arrived but Renfei's seat remained empty.

"She's flushing her cyanide pill down the toilet," Lu told them. That sent them back to their seats, whispering to each other behind their hands.

The professor proposed to keep his opening remarks brief, assuming that the prize-winner would like to say something and, as this was the last class of the semester, discussion could be expected to take longer. His topic was The Right To Intervene and he was proposing to argue for international intervention inside state borders. It was a subtle argument, full of nuances, because the intervention he proposed was not military invasion by a powerful state or coalition but intervention by international civil society. It was not military boots on the ground that protected human rights in the contemporary world, he believed, but prying eyes, technical expertise, medical and humanitarian support and legal resources capable of bringing political leaders before international courts and tribunals.

Renfei arrived. She was wearing her student uniform, a simple cotton dress in blues and yellows and the brown sandals with brass studs. She walked quickly to the vacant seat held by Lu, sat down, nodded to the professor and folded her hands on her lap. He was relieved she had been able to come. The media was still simmering with titbits from Liyong's scandalous visit and he understood why she had kept away, but he was glad now that she was back, taking her place in the class again. It had seemed empty without her.

He cleared his throat. "You are aware that I am announcing this evening the winner of the vice-chancellor's special prize for a foreign student. This is given each year to the student who effectively expresses in his or her work the nature of the contemporary world. It has been won in a wide range of disciplines – politics, law, economics, science, arts. This year's winner is from this class. I congratulate the class as a whole. It has been a pleasure and a privilege to be its teacher. One person gets the prize, but there is no doubt that the high level of class discussion has contributed."

He opened his remarks by noting that human rights had been in the background of international politics for centuries, as the rights of regional and ethnic groups against rulers, mostly monarchs and emperors, and the "rights of man" in support of the American and French revolutions in the 18th century. The 19th century had been relatively calm. The famous Concert of Powers kept things stable in Europe, if not in the colonies that the Europeans had collected. Human rights became prominent again in world politics after the Second World War, with the United Nations Universal Declaration of Human Rights, 1948. He did a quick survey of developments since then, emphasising bipartisan political support in Australia for the International Criminal Court (despite determined opposition from the United States), and then turned to his favourite subject, the state.

The (capitalised, he insisted) State was as potent and mysterious in political iconography as the Holy Ghost was in Christian theology (he drew on his little book for the pithy aphorism). Some saw it as the culmination of humanism, others as the source of tyranny. It was neither the nation nor the government – governments come and go, the nation was the people and the territory they occupied. Functionally, the State was a set of institutions, bureaucracy, legal system, armed forces and law enforcement agencies, inherited from the monarchs and emperors who needed them to maintain power. But it was another inheritance, sovereignty, that gave the State its potency, including the right to spy, tax and declare war, all in defence of its infallible right (as Machiavelli said) to survive. *L'etat, c'est moi*, attributed to Louis XIV of France, provided the essence of the idea.

And now, the most interesting (and risky) stage of his remarks – the ascent into the stratosphere of the barely tangible and not yet fungible contemporary world.

"The nature of the contemporary world, with global capitalism, digital technology and social media, active non-government organisations and now an international legal system to deal with mass atrocities, makes it increasingly difficult for states to hide abuse of power within their borders. As the world becomes aware, in real time, of abuses of human rights, more sophisticated ways of international intervention, short of invasion and war, are required. Intervention need not mean regime change, as military invasion almost certainly does."

He could see the girl Luci elevating her eyebrows, the rest of her face in an expression of boredom. Renfei's eyes were modestly downcast, her hands still folded. Jian seemed to be examining the far distance. Knut was staring at him, absorbing every word.

He felt a wave of compassion and sadness for the bright young people in his class, smart and smiling, alert to catch the latest fashion. When he was young, it was simple to be modern; clear thinking and uncluttered lines would replace the rococo past. Now, the world and its fashions were even more mix-and-match than the past he had left behind. He sometimes thought that global forces were gathering ominously, waiting for history's starting gun. In the marketplace of ideas it was marketing, not ideas, that held sway, and to market yourself you needed a smile and a titillating story or two. The Web and its bloggers had created a global audience of single-minded ideologues and single-issue fanatics. The more provocative and

179

unreasonable they were, the more attention they received. He wondered how long the bubble would last. Would not ignorance and dogma destroy the conversation of civilisation, just as meretricious art destroyed the art market and bad loans destroyed the stock market?

"And so on ..." he concluded abruptly, bringing a murmur of relief around the room. He took from an inside pocket a large envelope and brandished it, as if its existence established that everything was above board. He opened the envelope and extracted a piece of paper, which he appeared to be reading for the first time.

"And the winner is ... Knut Harkken!"

Knut was wearing a jacket, not because he knew he had won the prize but because he thought Renfei might be there with cameras hovering. He rose in his seat as if he had been sharply pinched in a tender part of his body. There was a round of applause, then a round of artificial groans.

"He doesn't need the money."

"Whether or not he needs the money, he has won the prize," the professor announced. "Because, in the opinion of the judges, he showed an understanding of the contemporary world in at least one particular respect. He understood that it is a creation of human beings. It is not some irresistible force, or immovable object, implanted by history or destiny, managed according to economic and political rules and regulations beyond the understanding of ordinary people. It is a human creation. And human beings can change it to meet human aspirations. Thank you, Knut!"

"And now," said the professor, moving aside in a show of humility, inviting Knut to join him, "Knut Harkken will respond to your appreciation and, of course, any questions."

Knut had something else in mind. "Was he really a spy?" he asked the professor, standing at his seat. He was asking the question everyone in the class wanted to ask.

While the professor gathered his wits, Knut pounced, raising his voice, playing to the gallery. "Do you think anyone in our class gave him info?"

The professor adopted his podium manner. There was an explanation for everything and every explanation could be expressed in language that everyone could understand.

"As to your first question, it is a well established principle of statecraft that the activities of agents are neither confirmed nor denied."

"The Chinese authorities in Australia have denied that he was working for them in any capacity whatsoever," Knut pointed out. "That's not neither confirming nor denying."

"There are different forms of plausible deniability," the professor said.

"You mean a blanket denial here in Australia, but pick him up for another job when he gets back to China?" Knut was determined to get it right.

"Something like that," said the professor.

"Who paid his fare to Australia?" asked Knut. "And who paid his fare back?"

"That no doubt will be tomorrow's story," remarked the professor.

"Yes, but what's your answer?" Knut was like a dog with a bone. He had no sense of the way things were done. He wouldn't have been given the prize if the professor had knocked him off the short list, but he didn't care.

"Why should I know something like that?" The professor tried to seem modest in his ignorance.

"Some people think the university staged it, in a deal with the government." Groans of dissent mixed with murmurs of excitement, but Knut was unsparing. "And some people think the television show, run by a relative of yours, brought him to Australia."

The professor remembered how at Mrs Winterbourne's dinner party Renfei had confessed to being bothered by "conflictual scenarios" on the Web. He looked at her now in the hope of a glimpse of reassuring sanity.

"I don't think a university class is the right place to bother about every bit of nonsense on the Web," he said.

"Unless it's true," said Knut. Success had not spoiled him. He was his usual irritating self. He would spare no one in his search for something he could call the truth.

"And what about my other question?"

"Which was?"

"Did anyone in this class give him info?"

"That's a nice little research project for you, Knut," said suave Professor Ian Ferrier.

"Why don't you ask the leading lady for her version?" Knut demanded.

The professor decided it was time for him to take charge. "She's had enough public attention for the moment."

"Perhaps she is saving her story for the tabloids," said the indomitable, prize-winning Knut Harkken from Norway. He smiled at Renfei as if they were still friends.

The professor gathered his papers, indicating closure. "Thank you, Knut, for that instructive interlude." His tone was aloof, but he refrained from making quotation marks in the air to enclose "instructive interlude" in absurdity. He paused, unwilling to leave the last word with Knut, and then decided to make a sweeping statement.

"Your generation faces the greatest threat to human rights in human history."

The class was silent, unable to reconfigure itself as a topic for discussion.

"You will recall our analysis earlier in the year of the different kinds of intelligence gathering, humint, or human intelligence, and sigint, signals intelligence, or technical interception. I would be relieved if Liyong's visit were evidence that China is engaging in human intelligence. If Liyong was a spy, he was indeed human. Fancy thinking that what is said in this class – what I say! – is important enough to be reported back to the powers that be in Beijing."

That got a warm response, so he continued. "I repeat. Your generation faces the greatest threat to human rights in human history."

"When women have all the top jobs," an Australian voice declared, to roars of male approval.

"When the mass invasion of privacy by the State, in the name of national security, is coupled with the mass intrusion on privacy by the social media, in the name of the free market, you have a perfect storm. Think if they got their lines crossed. Think bribery and corruption on a grand scale."

But the mind of the class, as mysterious and potent as the State and the Holy Ghost, was fixed on another kind of threat.

"The tyranny of female charm," someone shouted.

"Better than the iron oligarchy of male chauvinism," someone shouted back.

"A friend in power is a friend lost. Henry Adams." That took a while to digest.

"Only the impotent are pure. Gough Whitlam." Applause!

The professor waited until the class had exhausted its reserves of wit. He was considering a flippant remark that would somehow protect Renfei, when he noticed that the four friends were gathering their belongings and consulting their watches, probably arranging to meet for a celebratory drink for Knut.

His concern was misplaced. They would survive.

"I love the early morning time, don't you?"

"Well ..." was the professor's considered response.

They were meeting for the last time, at café bar 181, before Renfei returned to China. It was blustery and they went inside, to Gillian's favourite spot at the far end, near a wall of coloured brick, with a box of bamboo shoots and a mirror over their table. He was dressed for unimportant public engagements, navy jacket, striped shirt, open collar, grey slacks. Renfei was wearing a tweed jacket and a red woollen scarf. She looked attractive in red, Ian thought, especially when her lips were red as well. She had applied lipstick liberally. Often she did not use it at all; then her lips were pale and moist. Red brought out the honest energy in her face. She looked like early pictures of Mao Zedong, the revolutionary poet.

"People are cheerful in the morning, because they have a purpose, don't you think?"

"Like getting through the day," said the professor, dry lips turned down.

"You are not lacking in cynicism." Renfei felt able on her last day to treat him as an old friend being left behind.

"Just honest," he said. "For most people, life's purpose is elusive."

Renfei toyed with the word "elusive", settling into her seat with a show of satisfaction. "They may not be brimming with purpose, but they are happy to be doing something." She, at any rate, was cheerful.

"You sound like Marty Morewitz," said the professor. "The cheerful chatter of supply and demand." He contemplated another prospect. "Some would rather stay curled up in bed."

"Do you curl up in bed, professor?"

He was reminded of the time in his office when she had pirouetted to the door. "Shall we dance?" And her kiss in the gardens.

"That reminds me," he began, unable to avoid a twist of his lips that might, seen through critical eyes, be a smirk, and then hesitated, brushing aside with a flick of one hand whatever it was he had been reminded of. "What will you do in China? I mean, what kind of job will you be looking for? If I can help with a reference, you'll let me know, of course."

"I haven't decided."

No, he thought, you are only interested in who you are, not what you do. You are in for a rough time. You will either help to run the country or you will be out on your ear, a brooding dissenter somewhere in Europe or the United States. Or a recluse in a mountain cave outside Lijiang.

"Well, it will be good to see your parents again."

Renfei gathered herself. She had prepared her parting thoughts. She did not want him to think that she was returning to China because she didn't like Australia. On the contrary, she had learned a lot during her time here. Also, she could not leave without telling him how much she appreciated the help he and his family had given her. The kindness of the Winterbournes had been "belligerent". She had been given a glimpse of Australia's "elite thinking", through meeting the professor's family. "I am devoted to eccentric persons," she said.

"I did not know how to give a parting present. Everything seemed less than not enough." Then it had hit her, like "a bolt from nowhere". She would return the little red car.

"It has a new life now. When Mr Winterbourne sees it in the garage, he will not think sadly about his daughter. He will remember all the pleasure it gave me, his adopted daughter from China, which shares the Pacific Ocean with Australia."

Her smile was warm and open and the professor's mind sent a message to his heart. His stepfather's emotional state was for him an even more remote prospect than the emotional state of Mrs Winterbourne, but Renfei made it seem normal. She was the only person he knew who did not make fun of Charlie Boy.

"I thought you might have given it to your friend Lu."

"Lu can't drive and she won't learn because she likes to be a passenger."

Their orders arrived in the hands of a young Asian woman in white pants and black shirt – coffee and muffin for her, tea and toasted raisin bread for him. Renfei became nervous when she was served by someone who might be a foreign student. The professor behaved as if the serving girl did not exist, and Renfei did her best, short of disowning him, to indicate that she and the girl had as much, perhaps more, in common than she had with the man who might be paying the bill. She did this by friendly eye contact and assisting with wiping the table and placing utensils.

"So China's soft power got you in the end." They looked at each other with open, searching eyes.

"You can say that," she said, "but I am making a return to China for other reasons." She paused before her pronouncement. "Life is too easy in Australia."

The professor adopted his droll face. "Over the years, I've heard a range of reasons from students for returning home – and for staying – but that's the first time anyone has said life here was too easy."

"I am in love with Australia," Renfei said defiantly. She loved the brisk weather, which was "sportive", the clean air, which was "hopeful", the shops and markets, which were "beckoning", the trams, parks and gardens, all of which were "healthful", and the people, who were "making themselves into something else". Australia was truly cosmopolitan, people from all over the world fitting in together. The four friends had been to the Moomba Festival on the banks of the Yarra and Jian had said it was like Urumchi in the old days, only cleaner.

"You need not be just another nation like everyone else," Ms Liu advised the professor. "You can be a laboratory for fitting people in." She became inventive. "Dark, handsome men, as in movies from Turkey, and women from Sweden with long blonde hair. Asians and Africans. And Aboriginal people who have their own land and listen to the wind in the trees."

There were many "diversions" in Australia, so many groups, ethnic and cultural, social and economic, intellectual and religious, that it was possible to choose one and fit comfortably into it (she actually said "snuggle" into it), not paying attention to what was going on in the rest of society.

In China, it was not possible, unless you were wealthy or lawless. You had to take account of the broad consensus ("live in the middle of the big picture" were her words) and, if you did not agree with it, accept the consequences, whatever they were. They might be heavy, like going to jail, or they might be light, like not being able to get the job you want or being a social outcast, but they were inevitable.

"In Australia, you can spend your life thinking about how to be kind to animals," she said. "Or is a foetus a person?" These were not pressing questions. The world's people were concerned about where the next meal came from or whether they could be protected against diseases or how to give their child a chance to be educated. In China, also.

"In Australia, it is like a supermarket; you do not have to make big decisions, only lots of little ones." Her searching look returned. "You said it was a step forward to hold conflicting ideas in your head at the same time?" She wanted to be absolutely sure on this point. "You did, didn't you?"

"Yes," said the professor. "I did."

"But it was just a step. You said to be mature you had to resolve the conflict." She examined him intently. "You did, didn't you?"

"Yes, I did. To believe in contradictory ideas at the same time is what George Orwell called Doublethink. Peace is War!"

Renfei had not read George Orwell, but she liked the sound of him. "Well, I have decided. If I want to be mature, I have to return to China." She wriggled her shoulders, then shrugged them with cheerful resignation. "In China everything is there at once. You have to know yourself inside and outside."

The professor was not sure Australia was as diverse or as permissive as she thought. "As a foreign student in Australia, you have been in a privileged position." He declined her protest. "I don't mean money." He explained that many Australians were interested in the same big questions that bothered the people of China.

She nodded sombrely. "Australia is a kind of developing country. It is remarkable to think that just a few hundred years ago, it was ..." Renfei paused, unable to think of a description of Captain Cook's arrival that did not insult the Aboriginal people, "... untouched."

But there was something she needed to tell the professor. In anticipation, she allowed herself a sly smile. "I am also going back to China because I was reminded of something when Liyong was here."

"Yes," said the professor.

"The sexual experience is joyful." Detecting resistance, or indifference, she continued quickly. "If I am going back to China to struggle to get everything right inside, and outside as well, it would be good to be joyful, don't you agree?"

The professor nodded. "You have become wise. I cannot say the same for myself." She put her hand over his on the table. "You taught me so much."

He had always wanted Renfei to return to China, he realised, from the time they first met. He had thought it was personal: if she stayed in Australia, he might "do something". But it was something else. What he loved about Renfei was her courage. You needed courage to persist with learning, trying to understand. Otherwise, you just repeated what you were told, passed exams, got your meal ticket and went out into the world. Renfei had what used to be known as character. Her denial of Liyong, when she was in love with him, was proof of it. She would have denied the vice-chancellor, too, if he, Ian Ferrier, had been stronger. If she stayed in Australia, pursuing the good life, she would lose her moral core. She might finish up on television, smiling at everyone and waving her hands about. Australia was not worth it.

There, he had said it! The reviewers of his little book were right.

"Will you be getting in touch with Liyong?"

"I was not intending to adopt that procedure," said Ms Liu Renfei. She probed his eyes for confirmation of something she needed to know before she took leave of Australia, but he also needed to know something.

"Was he a spy?" the professor asked.

"I think so." She cocked her head to one side, alert and cooperative.

"How can you be sure?"

"The lonely boy pretending to be James Bond was not truthful," she said.

The professor deliberated. He did this by drawing geometrical forms on a napkin.

"Many things are said in private," he said, "especially by two people who are, as they say these days, a unit. But in a court of law, or even of public opinion, there is a need of evidence that is more substantial." He was unable to avoid again the suspicion of a smirk. "Substantial in the sense of being subject to corroboration that is lacking when one person confides in another between the sheets, in a manner of speaking."

Renfei had understood sufficiently to get his point, even without the smirk. "He made no secret of it. He asked me to do things."

The professor seemed relieved, although he continued his line of questioning. "Was your friend Lu with you when he asked? Or anyone else?"

"No. But he was different. His eyes had changed."

The professor deliberated again, this time by lowering his head and moving it from side to side. "I wondered," he said. "Of course, I knew, because you told me, that he was your boyfriend and had turned up in Melbourne."

"Yes."

"And I knew, because you told me, that he had asked you to inform on Chinese students in our class, and you had turned him down."

"Yes."

"But I realised, when the story broke all over the place ..." the professor threw up his hands, apologising with gestures for the indelicacy of the Australian media, "... that I had not taken into account the possibility that he was a Walter Mitty."

"Who is this Mitty?"

The professor described the ineffectual character of James Thurber's short story, who dreamed of himself in heroic situations. He observed that, in response to the "Liyong episode", the film with Danny Kaye was about to be revived in Melbourne.

"Was Mitty a Freudian?"

"Not consciously," said the professor.

"Is it possible to be a Freudian without knowing?" asked Renfei. "Like being a communist without believing in the dictatorship of the proletariat or being a Christian without believing that Jesus was the son of God."

Professor Ian Ferrier screwed up his face in a show of anguish. "Renfei, please. Not today." She gave a small internal smile of recognition of her role as dogged investigator of human ingenuity.

"You said you had not taken Mitty into account. When did you not do that?"

The professor, aware of the difficulty of proving or disproving a negative, proceeded anyway. He owed it to Renfei to be honest.

"When I told the vice-chancellor."

"What did you tell the vice-chancellor?"

"What you told me."

They looked at each other as if aware of real people for the first time.

"I wondered," said Renfei. "Whether you would tell someone else." She dropped her eyes.

"You are disappointed?"

"Yes."

"You didn't say it was in confidence. You knew the vice had asked me to help with campus security."

"Yes," said Renfei. "I almost knew."

"Well," said the professor, ignoring the reservation.

"I thought we were special friends. I thought we were understanding what was inside each other." She smiled wearily at an old memory.

"I'm sorry if I disappointed you," said Ian primly. "I had an obligation to keep the vice informed. I thought you understood that."

"Of course." Renfei seemed to be concluding the matter, but persisted, with her probing look. "I thought you didn't care whether the Chinese authorities knew what was said in class. We were free, speaking honestly. They might learn something, you said."

"Yes," said the professor. "That is what I said. That is what I think."

"Then why did you tell the vice-chancellor about Liyong?"

He was silent for quite a while, refusing to accept that he had betrayed her trust. "I had a duty of care." But she asked why his duty of care did not extend to her. "When the media people chased me, I thought I was a refugee," she said.

He reached across the table to take her hand. "I'm sorry, Renfei." Then he sat up, apparently satisfied. "Well, let's assume they were caught out. So they got someone to float the James Bond story."

Renfei shrugged her shoulders, with her "that's the way it was" look. "Never mind." She tossed her head, leaving her hand in his. "It's good Knut got the prize."

"He won it on merit. There were external examiners." The professor paused, on the brink of a sweeping statement, then decided to make it. "If it had been up to me, I would have given it to you."

He withdrew his hand and resumed his position as man of the world and caretaker of student welfare. Renfei's eyes were misty, her hand on the table where it had been deserted. She was thinking how different everything would have been if she had won the prize. Then she pulled her hand back and sat up straight.

"I have been shopping," said Ms Liu Renfei, her eyes sparkling. "I am taking back to China a filmy chemise."

She observed the deflating effect on him, but it was (she glanced at her watch) time for her to leave. She was meeting Lu and their friends, who were catching the bus with her to the airport for a "send up".

They stood up on either side of the little table. He allowed her to pass in front. He followed her down the long, narrow aisle, pausing to pay the cashier before pushing open the doors to the street. She was waiting for him on the footpath. Seeing her standing alone brought home to him that she was actually leaving, that perhaps he might not see her again.

"You will be careful, won't you?" He had a habit of brushing anything noticeable from the shoulders of a companion, which he did now. She smiled. "Of course." She could not stand his fussiness, yet it was heart-wrenching.

"Please remember me to your family, including Matthew and Verya, the to be newlyweds." She sounded like a maiden aunt. She brushed his cheek with her lips and took a few steps away. Then she turned and pirouetted.

He could not let her go without something to remember him by, a parting gesture she could recall when she was home again, embedded in China. He struggled to find words, but they would not come, and would be in any case inadequate. It came to him at that moment on the footpath outside café bar 181 that his former student was not only worthy of trust, but brave. He made a note in his head: the future of civilisation depended on finding a substitute for bravery in war.

So he stood erect, straightened his shoulders and saluted. As soon as he had done it, he felt foolish and stood with his head down, the offending hand resting on a round table top with an oriental pattern.

She accepted his gesture with a questioning inclination of her head, and then turned away, but suddenly reversed, running back to him, taking him in her arms. He could feel her body subside against his and he realised she was crying. He felt floods of joy and anguish. They stood together on the footpath, tearful in each other's arms. People passed respectfully around them with an occasional backward glance. Then gently, but deliberately, she disentangled herself and without looking back walked around the corner to the No 8 tram stop.

It was dogs and babies day. He stood for a while entangled in prams and leashes before turning to walk home. He knew, from the feel of the thought that was growing and occupying his mind, that he would have to become accustomed to it. It would not go away.

What would become of Ms Liu Renfei?

About the Author

AUSTRALIAN WRITER-DIPLOMAT BRUCE GRANT HAS written ten works of non-fiction, three novels, essays and short stories published in *The New Yorker*, *Mademoiselle*, *Playboy*, *Cleo*, *The Bulletin*, *Quadrant*, *Overland* and *Meanjin*. His first book, *Indonesia*, became a classic. *A Young Woman From China* is one of three novels on the theme "Love in the Asian Century". He was a Nieman Fellow at Harvard University, Australian High Commissioner in New Delhi, foundation chairman of the Australia-Indonesia Institute, chairman of the Australian Dance Theatre, chairman of the Victorian Premier's Literary Awards, president of Melbourne's International Film Festival and president of Melbourne's International Arts Festival. His essay "The Great Pretender at the Bar of Justice", written at the trial of Slobodan Milosevic, was published in *The Best Australian Essays 2002*. "Bali: The Spirit of Here and Now", written after the October 2002 bombings, was published in *The Best Australian Essays 2004*. He was awarded the degree of Doctor of Letters (*honoris causa*) by Monash University in December 2003 and distinguished Fellow by the Australian Institute of International Affairs in 2010.

www.ingramcontent.com/pod-product-compliance
Lightning Source LLC
Chambersburg PA
CBHW051834020726
47502CB00005B/1784